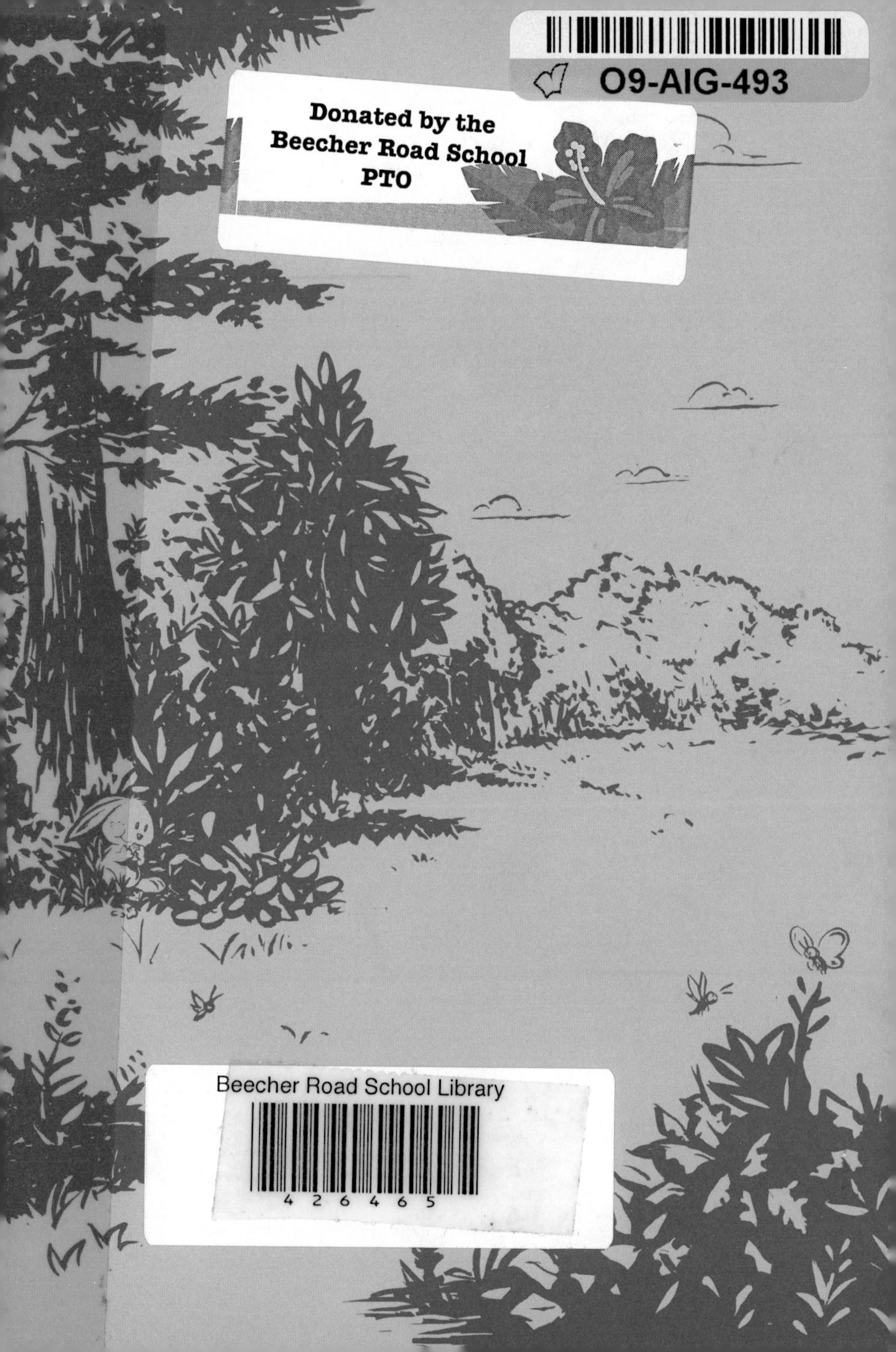

OWLY

JUST A LITTLE BLUE

ANDY RUNTON

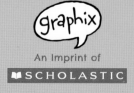

graphix

An Imprint of

SCHOLASTIC

All rights reserved. Published by Graphix, an imprint of Scholastic
Inc., *Publishers since 1920.* SCHOLASTIC, GRAPHIX, and associated logos
are trademarks and/or registered trademarks of Scholastic Inc.

The publisher does not have any control over and does not assume
any responsibility for author or third-party websites or their content.

Library of Congress Control Number: 2019947132

ISBN 978-1-338-30068-0 (hardcover)
ISBN 978-1-338-30067-3 (paperback)

10 9 8 7 6 5 4 3 2 1   20 21 22 23 24

Printed in China 62
First edition, September 2020
Edited by Megan Peace
Book design by Phil Falco
Publisher: David Saylor

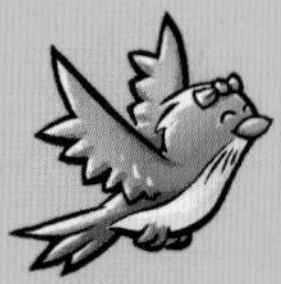

FOR MY MOM

FOR ALWAYS BEING
THERE FOR ME,
ESPECIALLY WHEN I
WAS A LITTLE BLUE

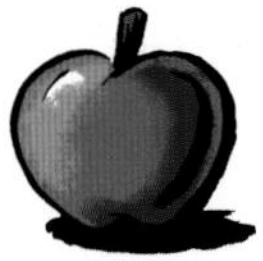

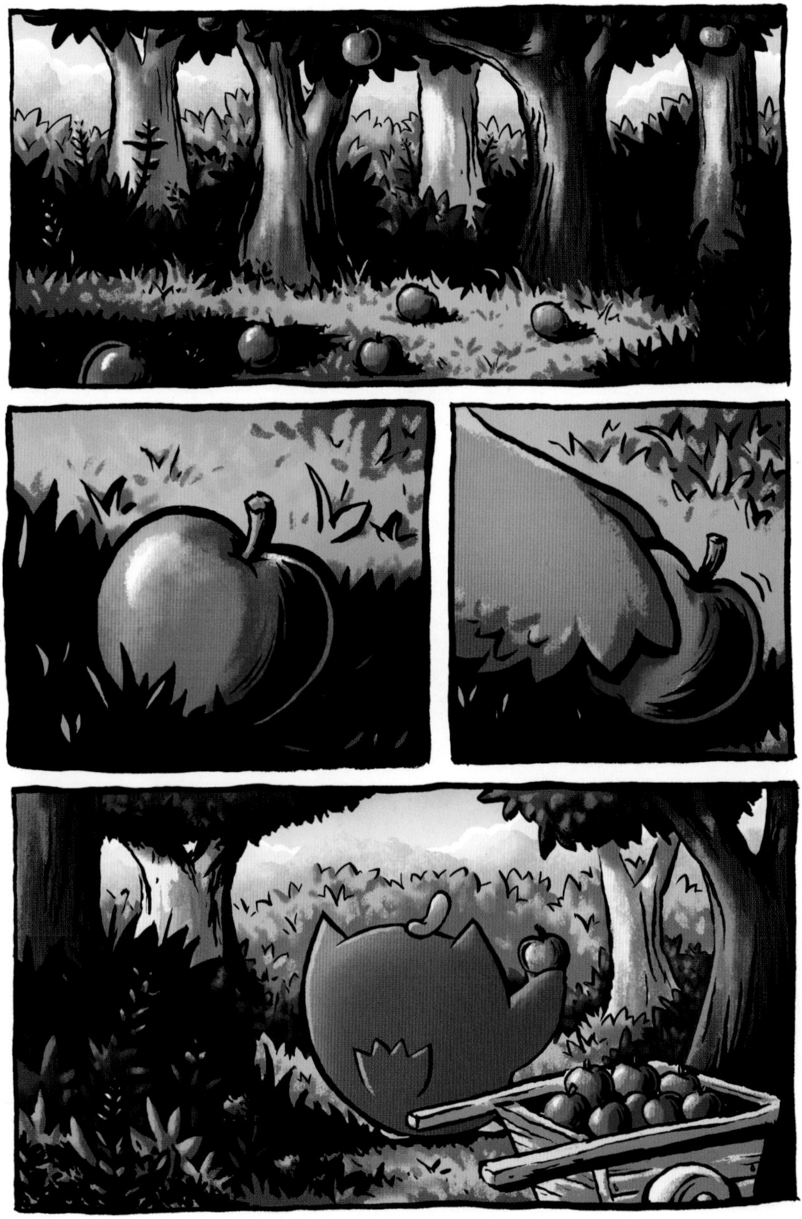

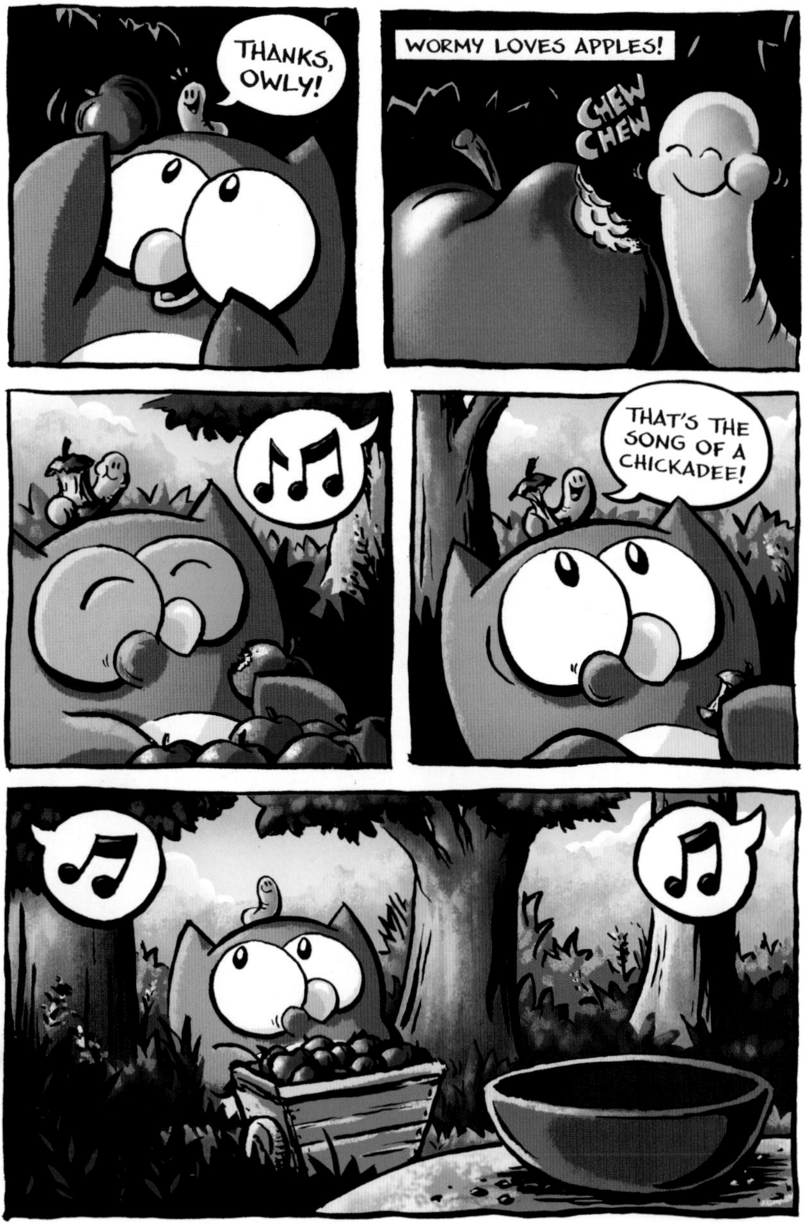
THANKS, OWLY!
WORMY LOVES APPLES!
CHEW CHEW
THAT'S THE SONG OF A CHICKADEE!

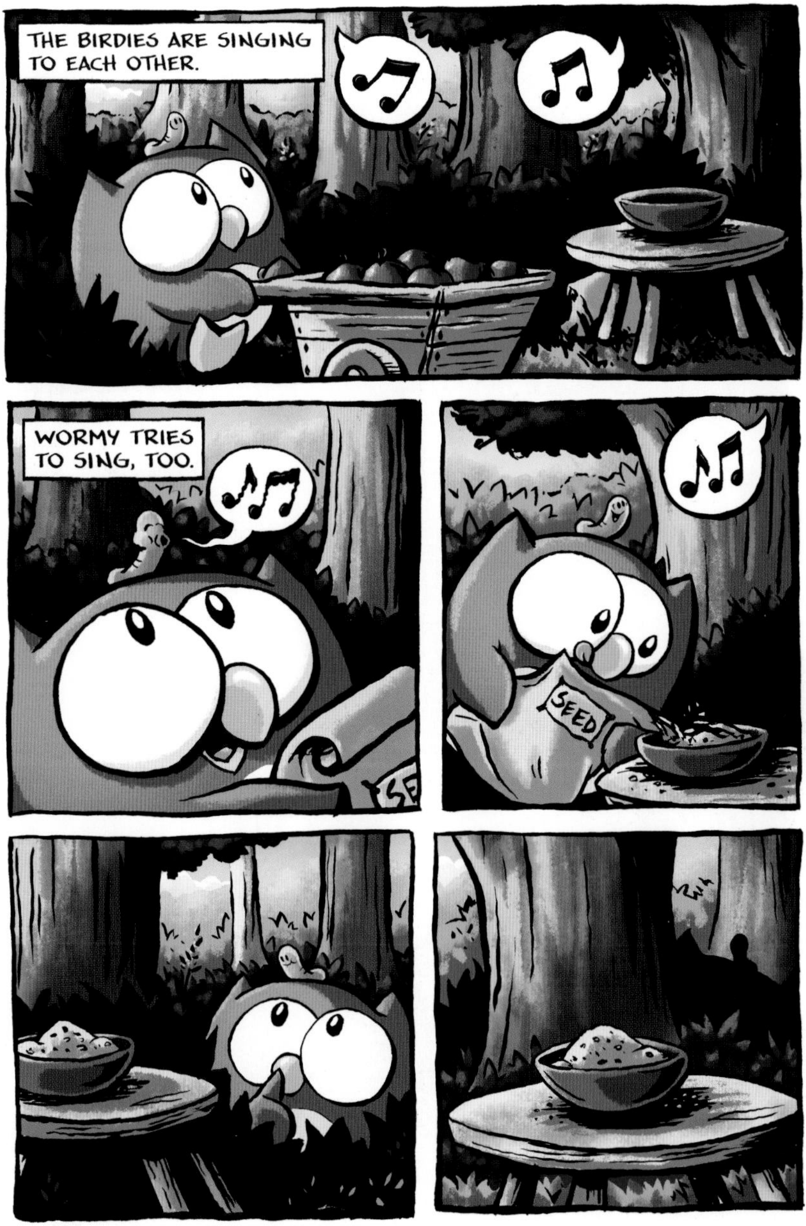
THE BIRDIES ARE SINGING TO EACH OTHER.
WORMY TRIES TO SING, TOO.
SEED

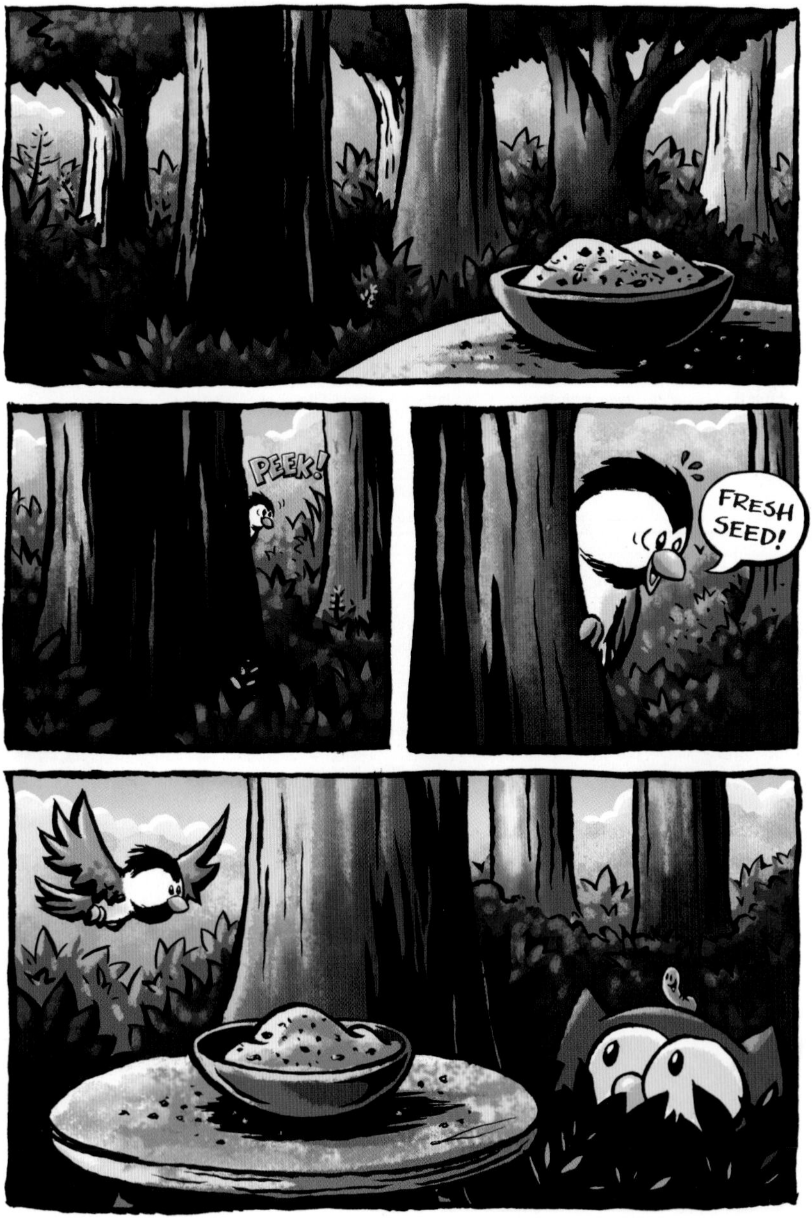
PEEK!
FRESH SEED!

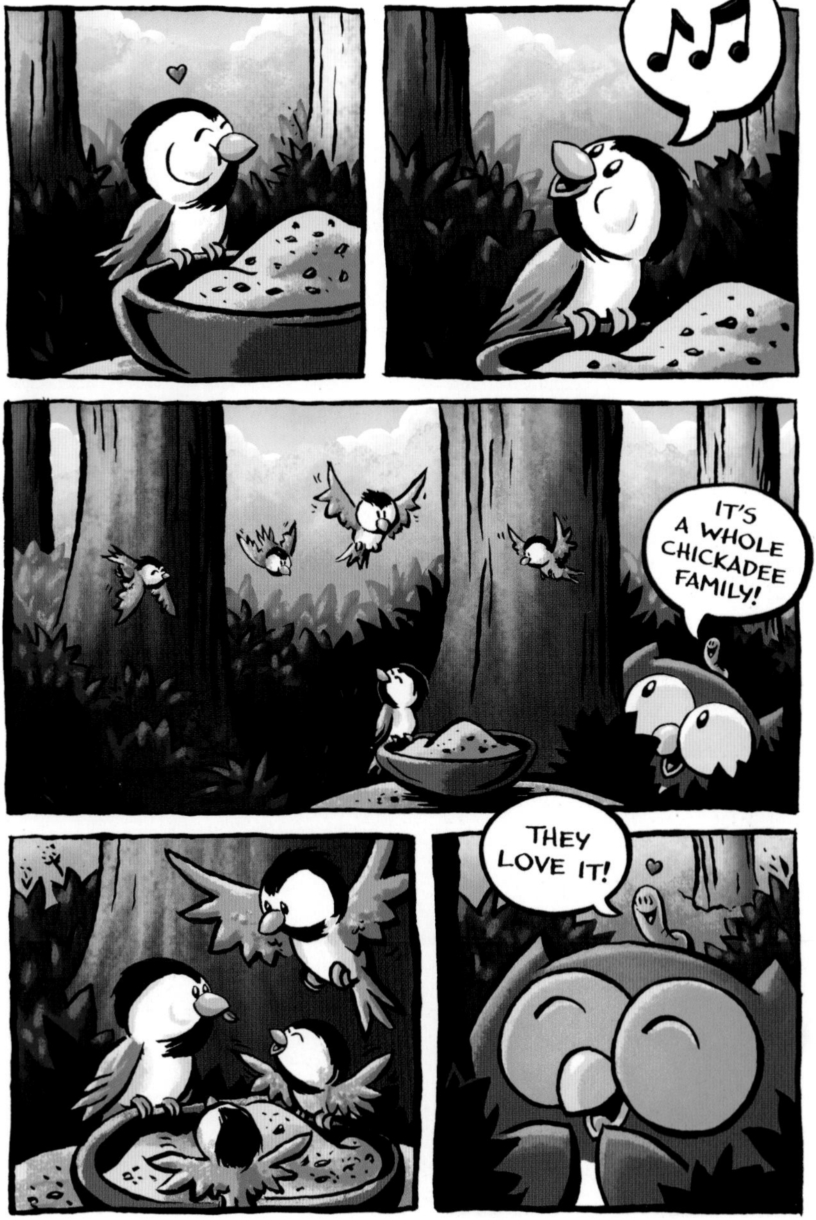
IT'S A WHOLE CHICKADEE FAMILY!
THEY LOVE IT!

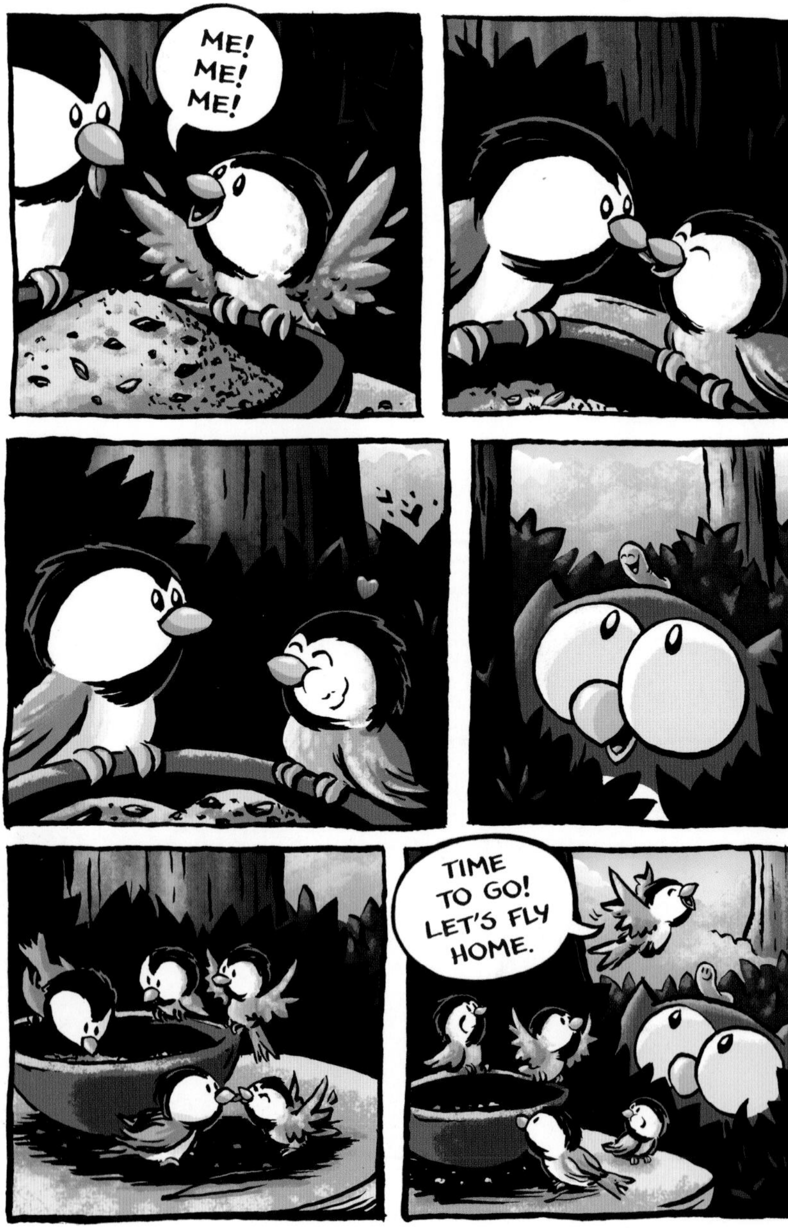
ME! ME! ME!
TIME TO GO! LET'S FLY HOME.

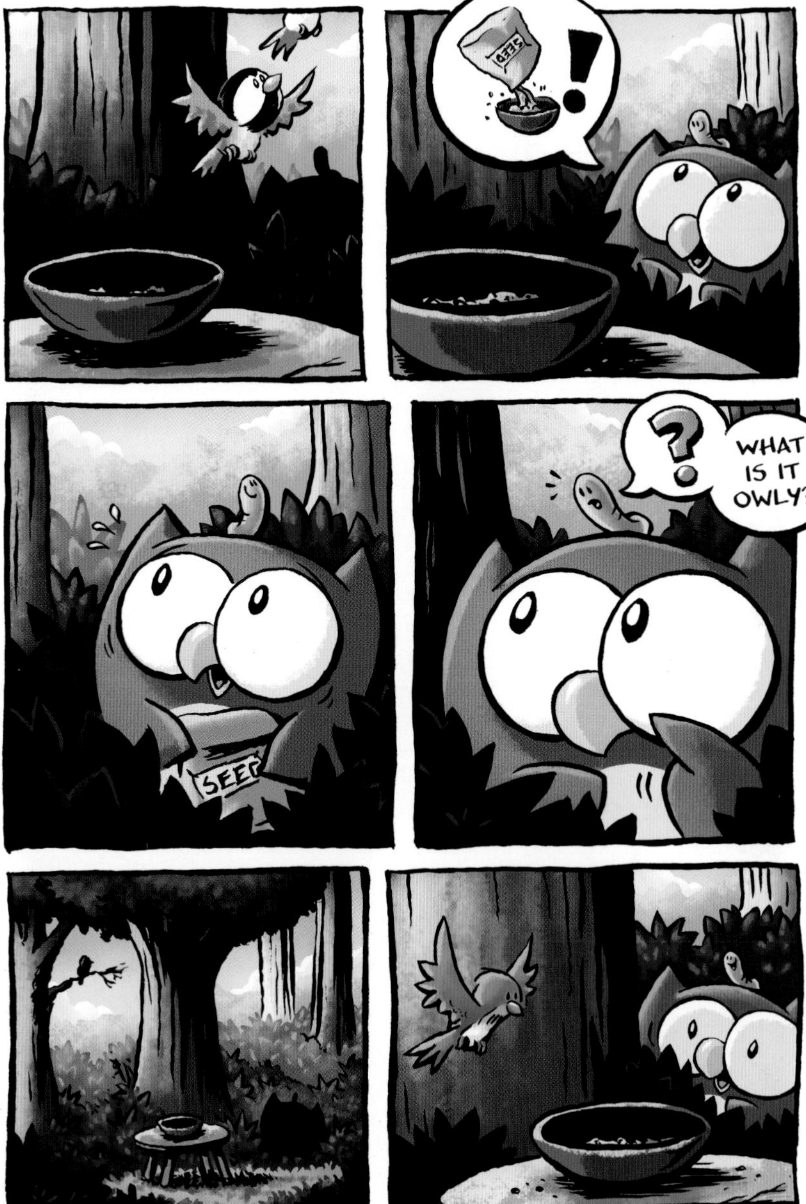
!
?
WHAT IS IT OWLY?

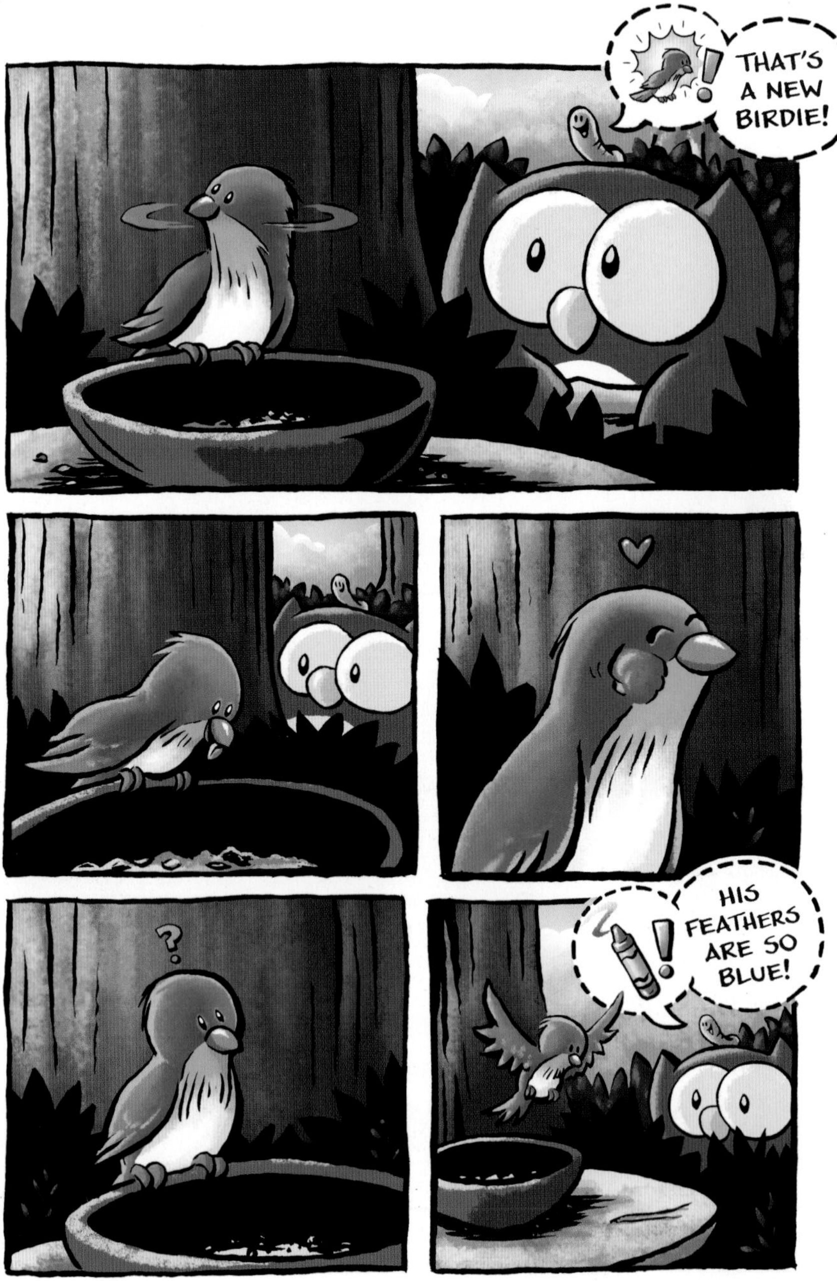
THAT'S A NEW BIRDIE!
HIS FEATHERS ARE SO BLUE!

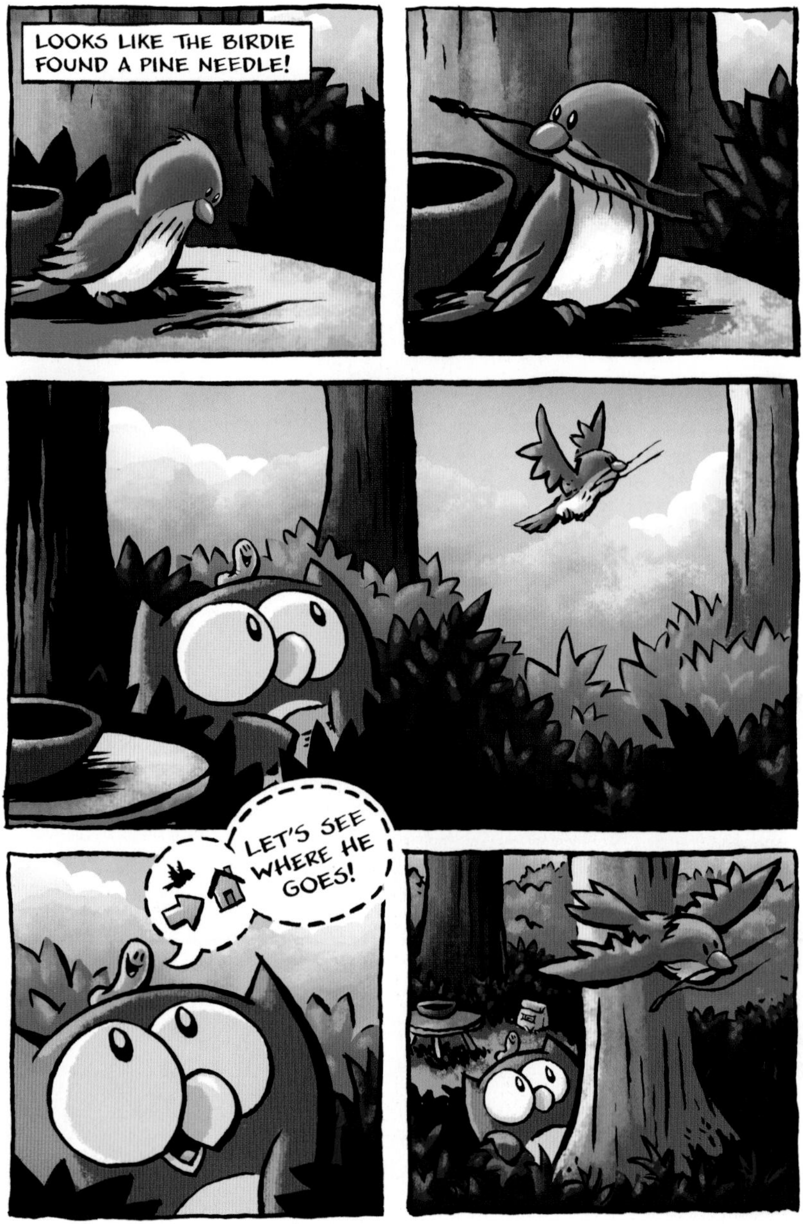
LOOKS LIKE THE BIRDIE FOUND A PINE NEEDLE!
LET'S SEE WHERE HE GOES!

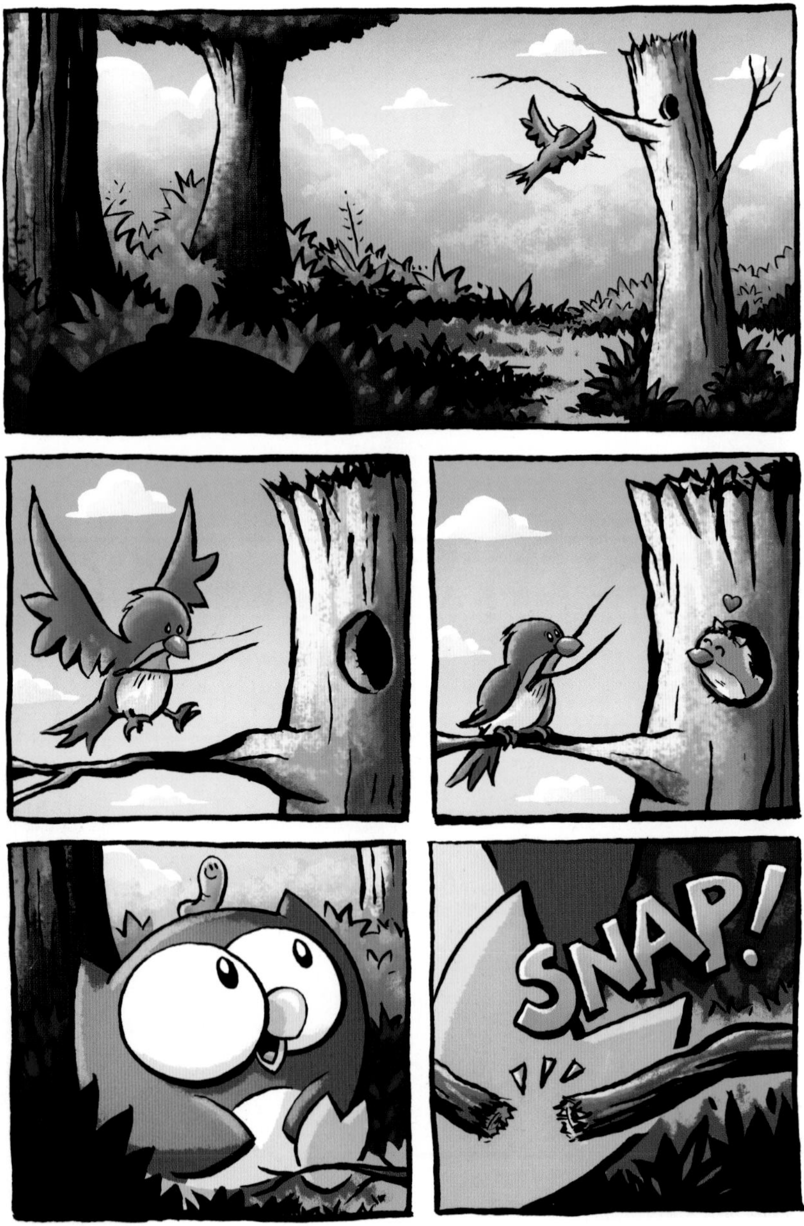
SNAP!

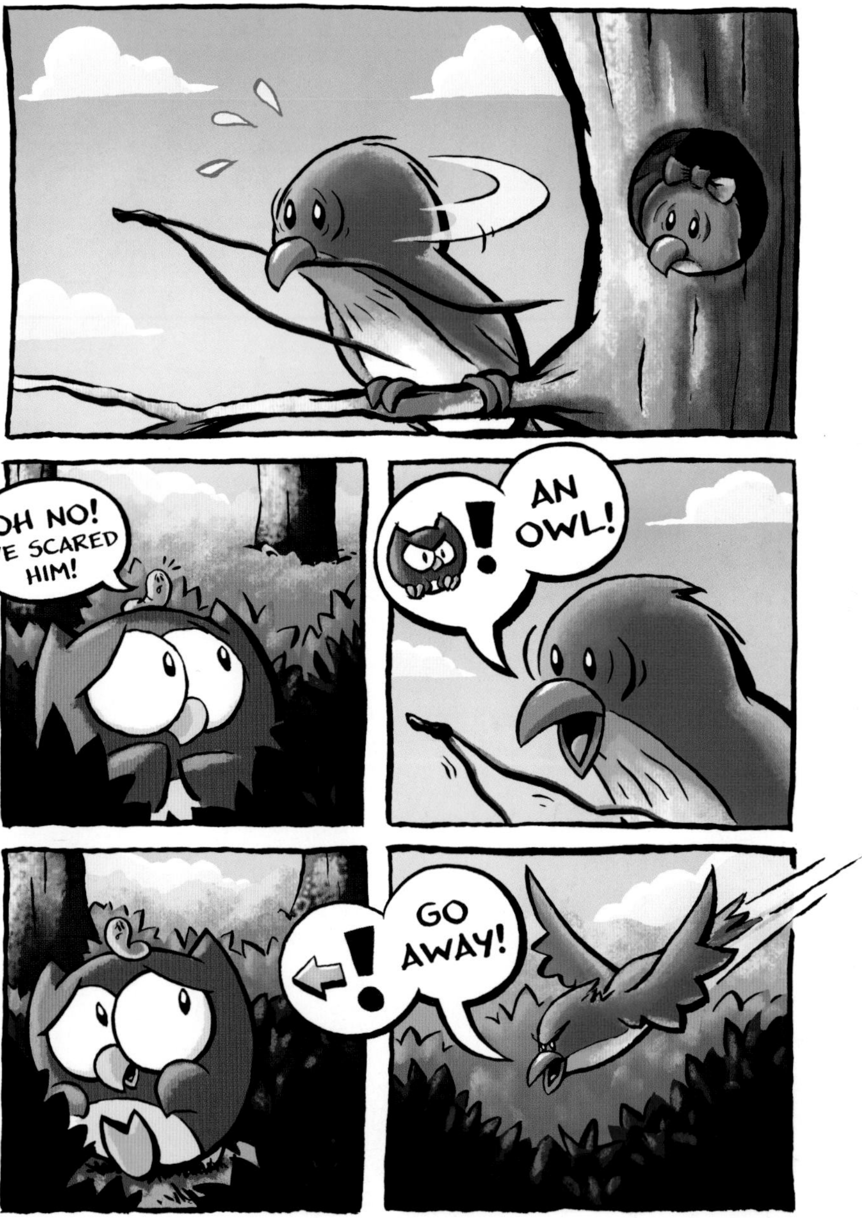
OH NO! WE SCARED HIM!
AN OWL!
GO AWAY!

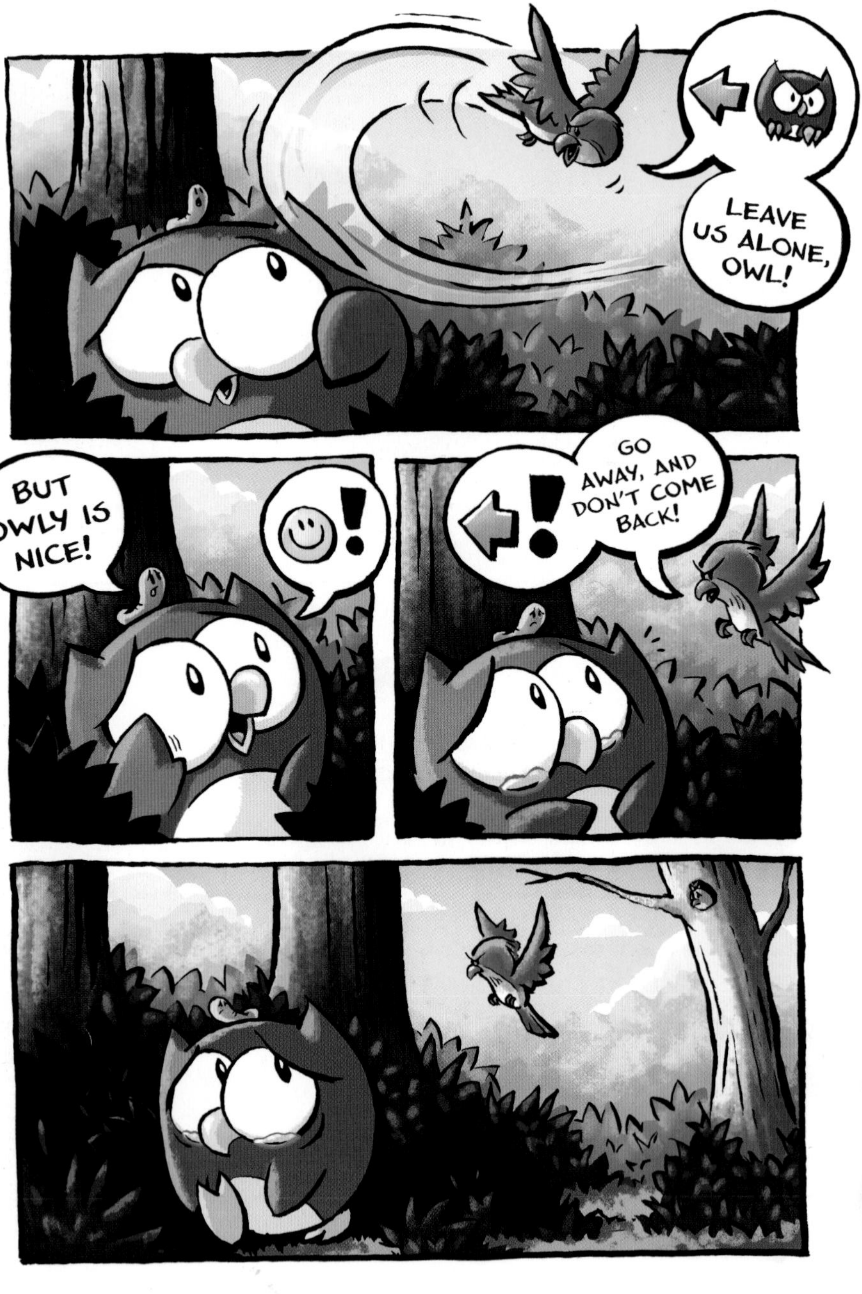
LEAVE US ALONE, OWL!
BUT OWLY IS NICE!
GO AWAY, AND DON'T COME BACK!

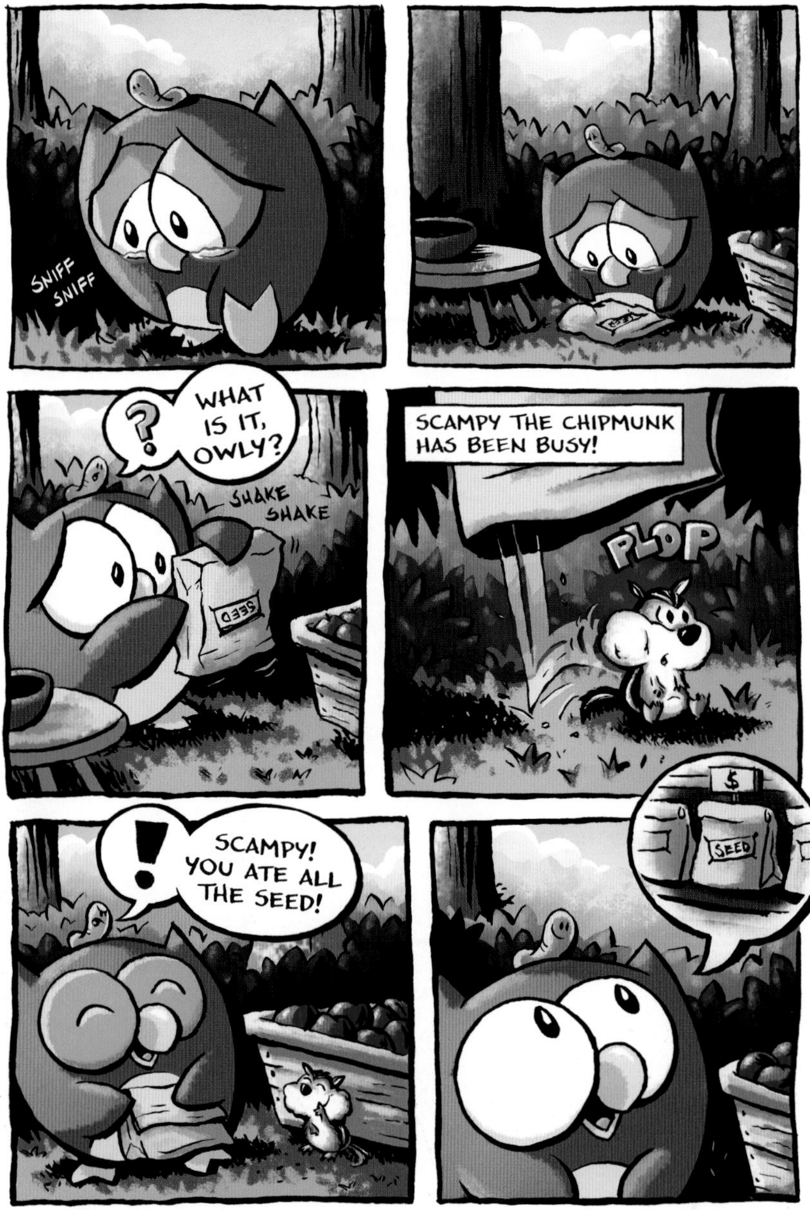
SNIFF
SNIFF
SEED
?
WHAT IS IT, OWLY?
SHAKE
SHAKE
SEED
SCAMPY THE CHIPMUNK HAS BEEN BUSY!
PLOP
!
SCAMPY! YOU ATE ALL THE SEED!
$
SEED

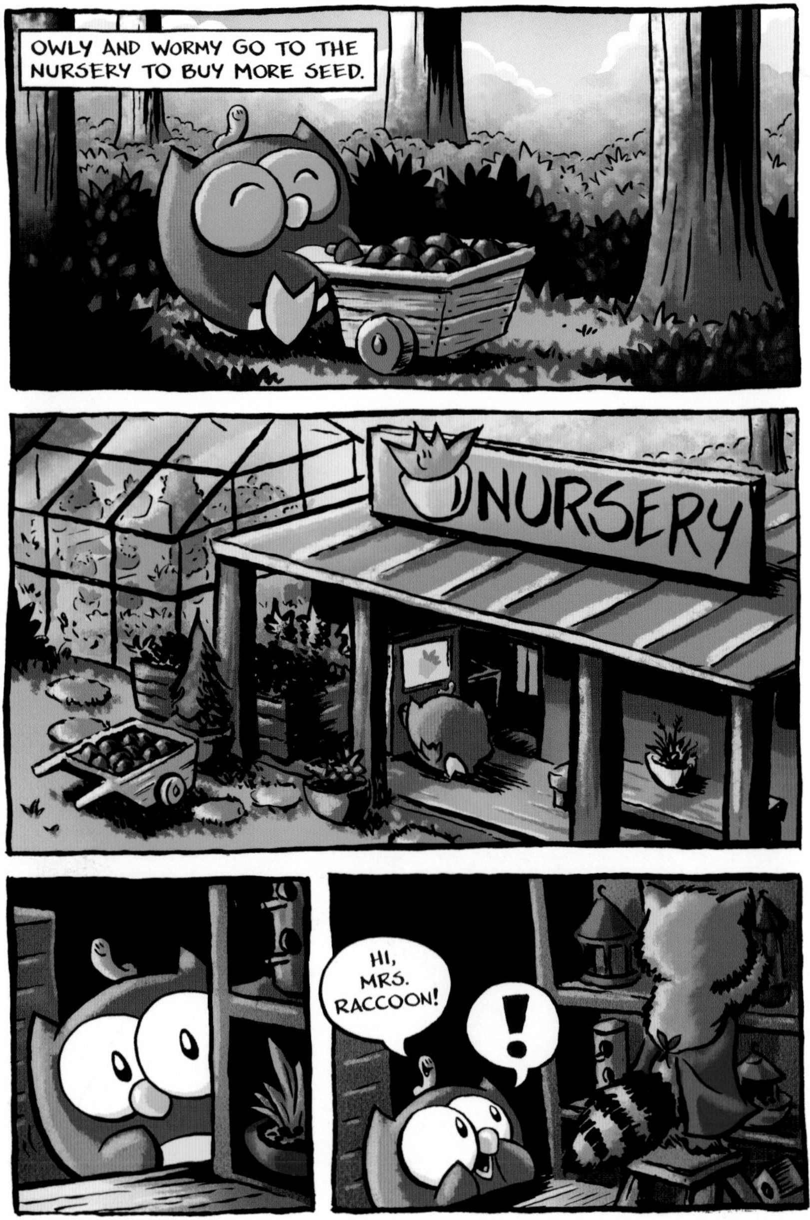
OWLY AND WORMY GO TO THE NURSERY TO BUY MORE SEED.
NURSERY
HI, MRS. RACCOON!
!

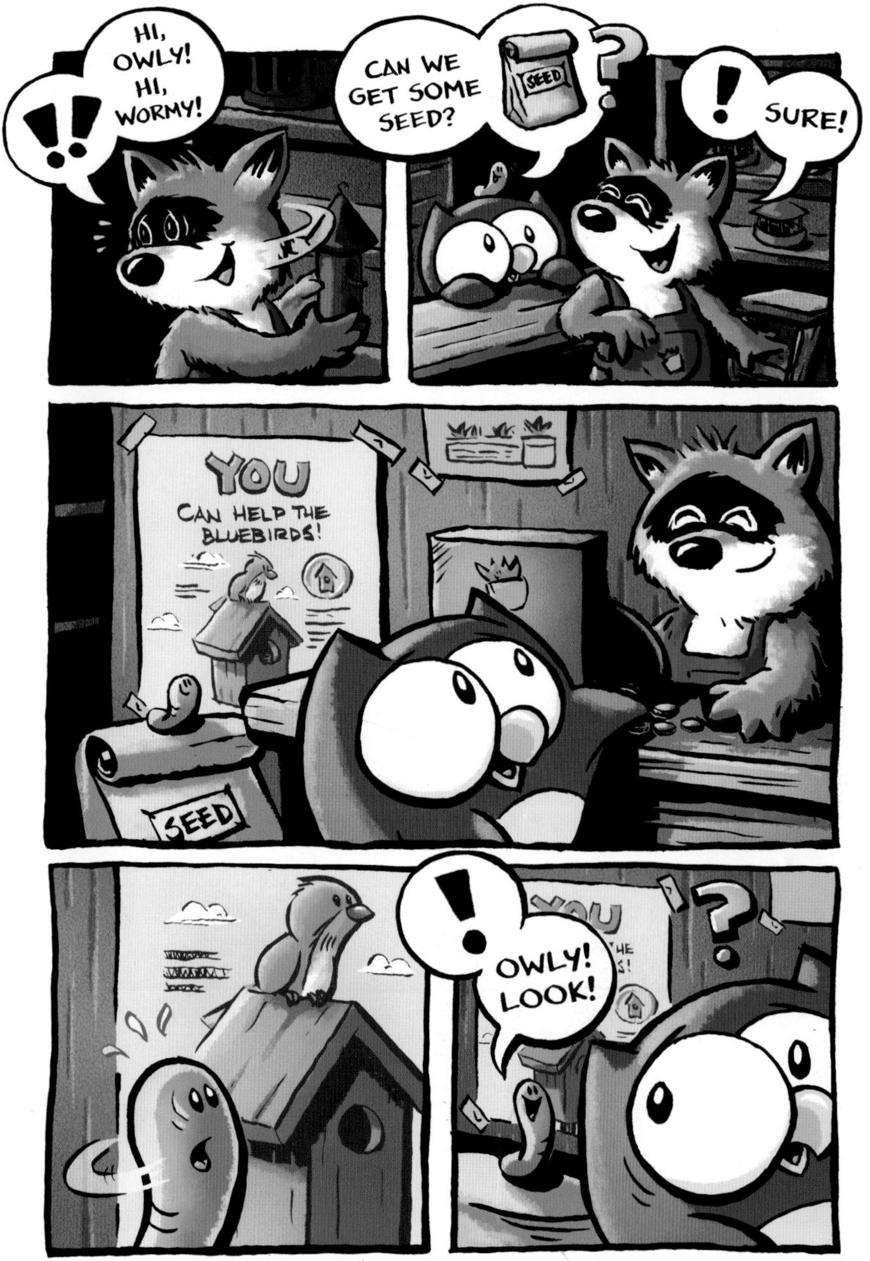
!!
HI, OWLY! HI, WORMY!
CAN WE GET SOME SEED?
SEED
?
!
SURE!
YOU
CAN HELP THE BLUEBIRDS!
SEED
!
OWLY! LOOK!
?

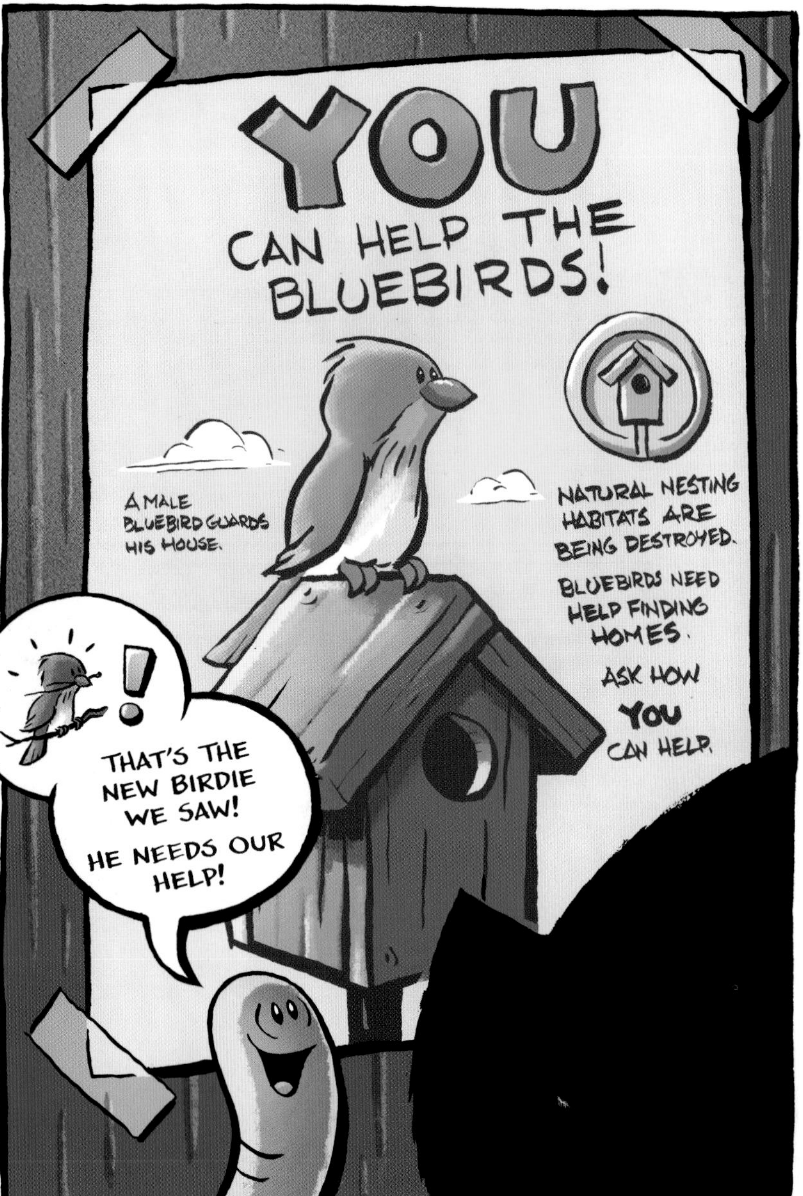
YOU
CAN HELP THE BLUEBIRDS!
A MALE BLUEBIRD GUARDS HIS HOUSE.
NATURAL NESTING HABITATS ARE BEING DESTROYED.
BLUEBIRDS NEED HELP FINDING HOMES.
ASK HOW YOU CAN HELP.
THAT'S THE NEW BIRDIE WE SAW!
HE NEEDS OUR HELP!

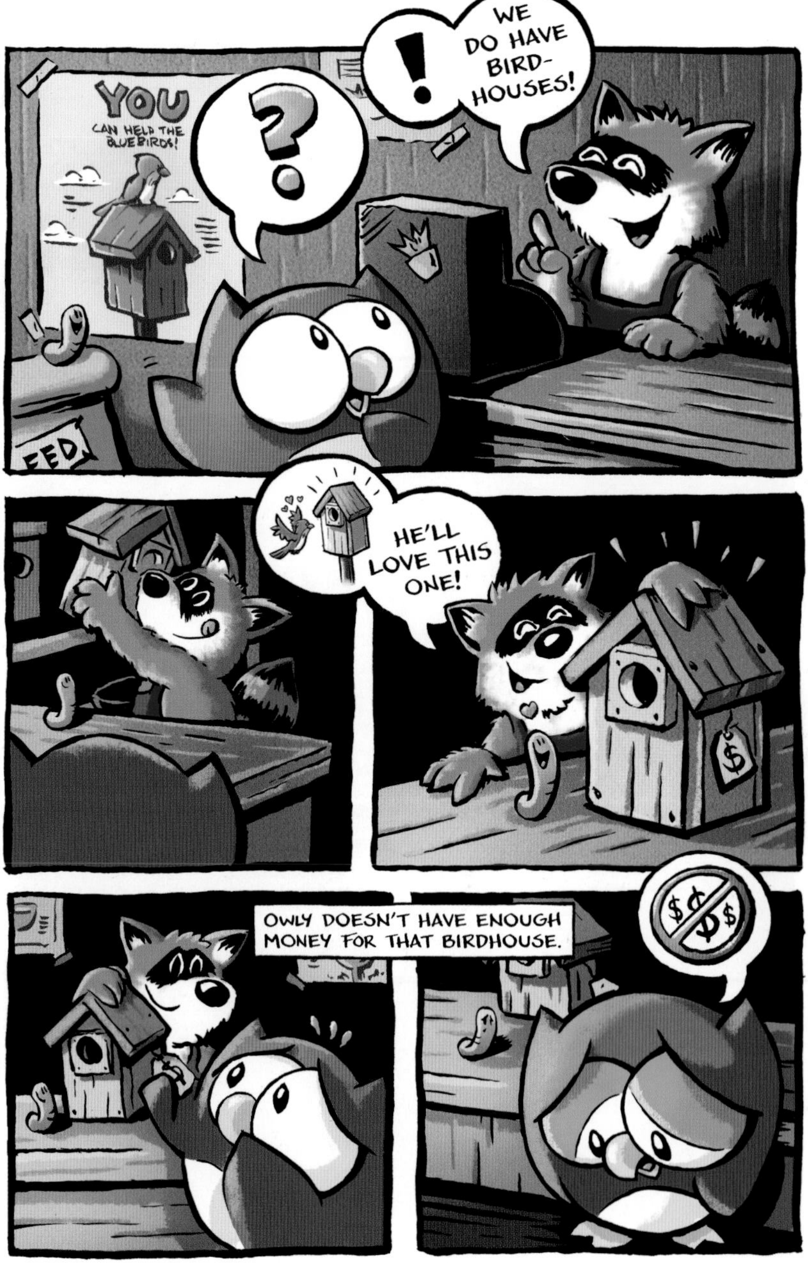
YOU
CAN HELP THE BLUEBIRDS!
?
!
WE DO HAVE BIRD-HOUSES!
FEED
HE'LL LOVE THIS ONE!
$
OWLY DOESN'T HAVE ENOUGH MONEY FOR THAT BIRDHOUSE.
$ $ $

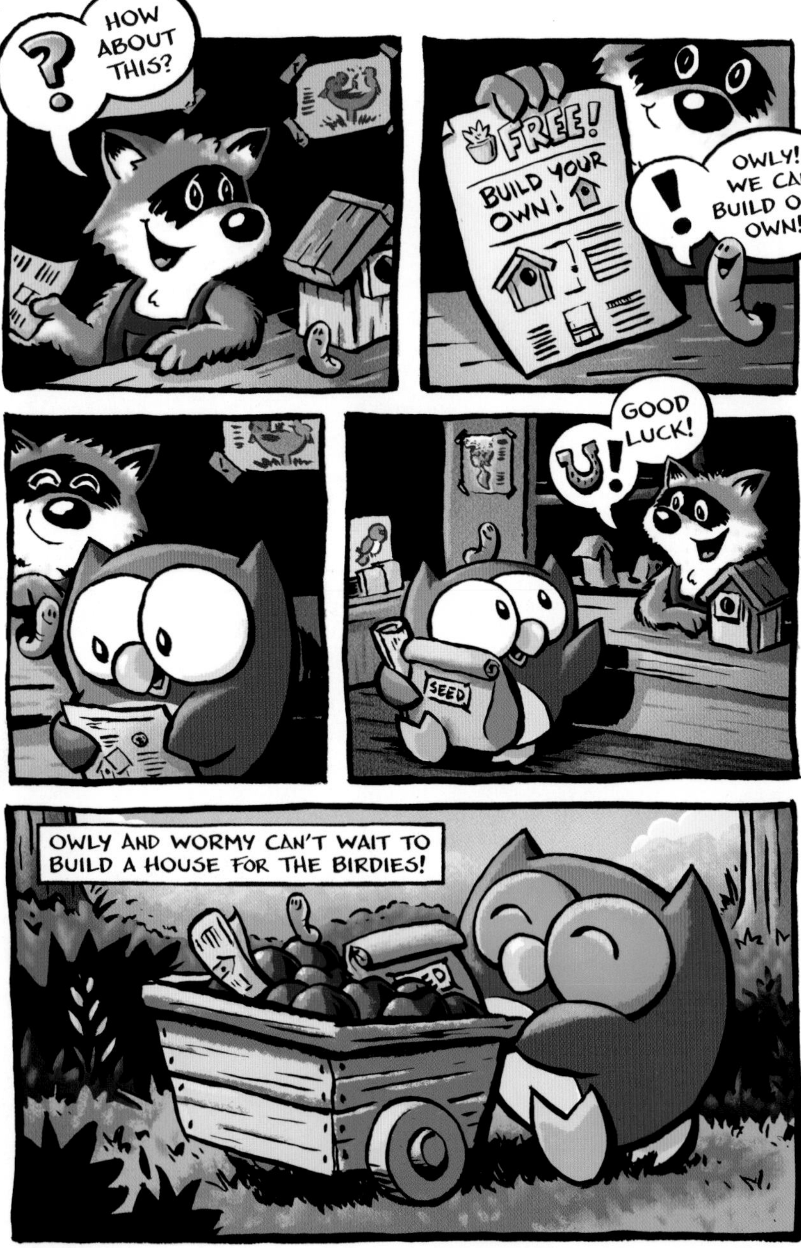
HOW ABOUT THIS?
FREE!
BUILD YOUR OWN!
OWLY! WE CAN BUILD OUR OWN!
SEED
GOOD LUCK!
OWLY AND WORMY CAN'T WAIT TO BUILD A HOUSE FOR THE BIRDIES!

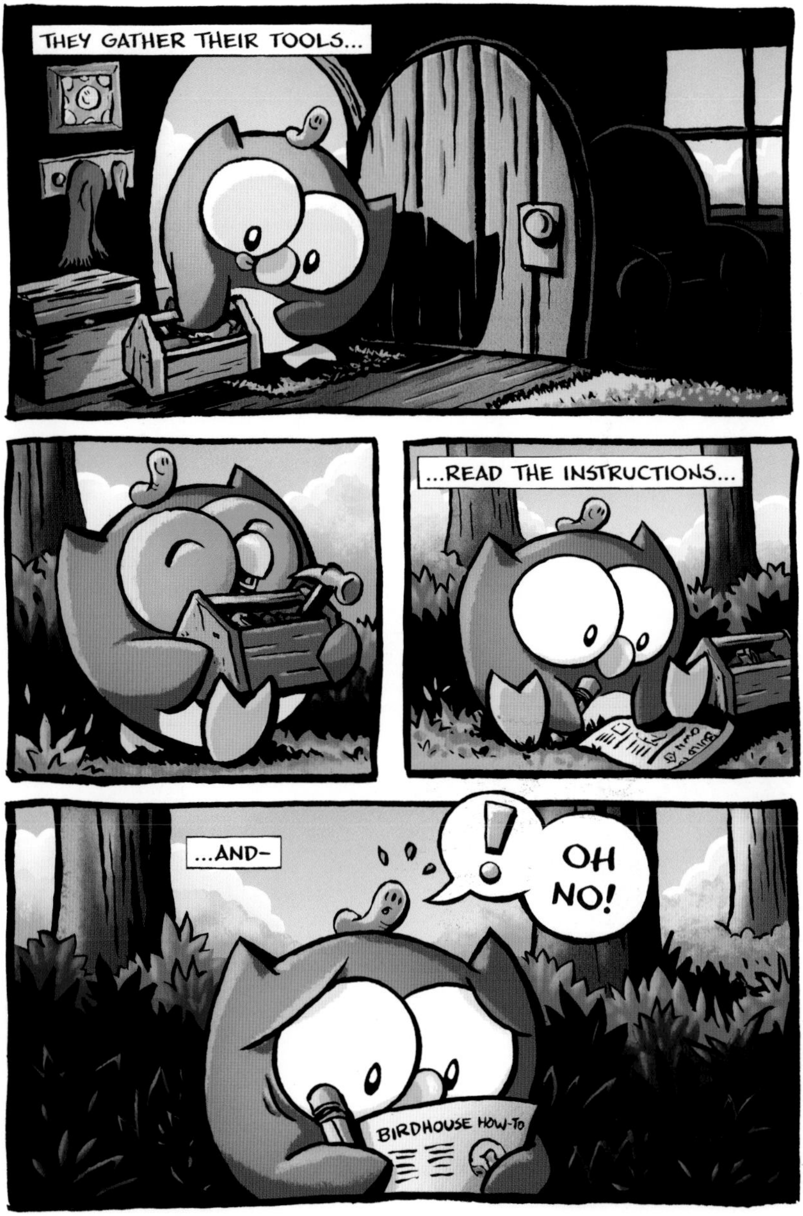
THEY GATHER THEIR TOOLS...
...READ THE INSTRUCTIONS...
...AND-
!
OH NO!
BIRDHOUSE HOW-TO

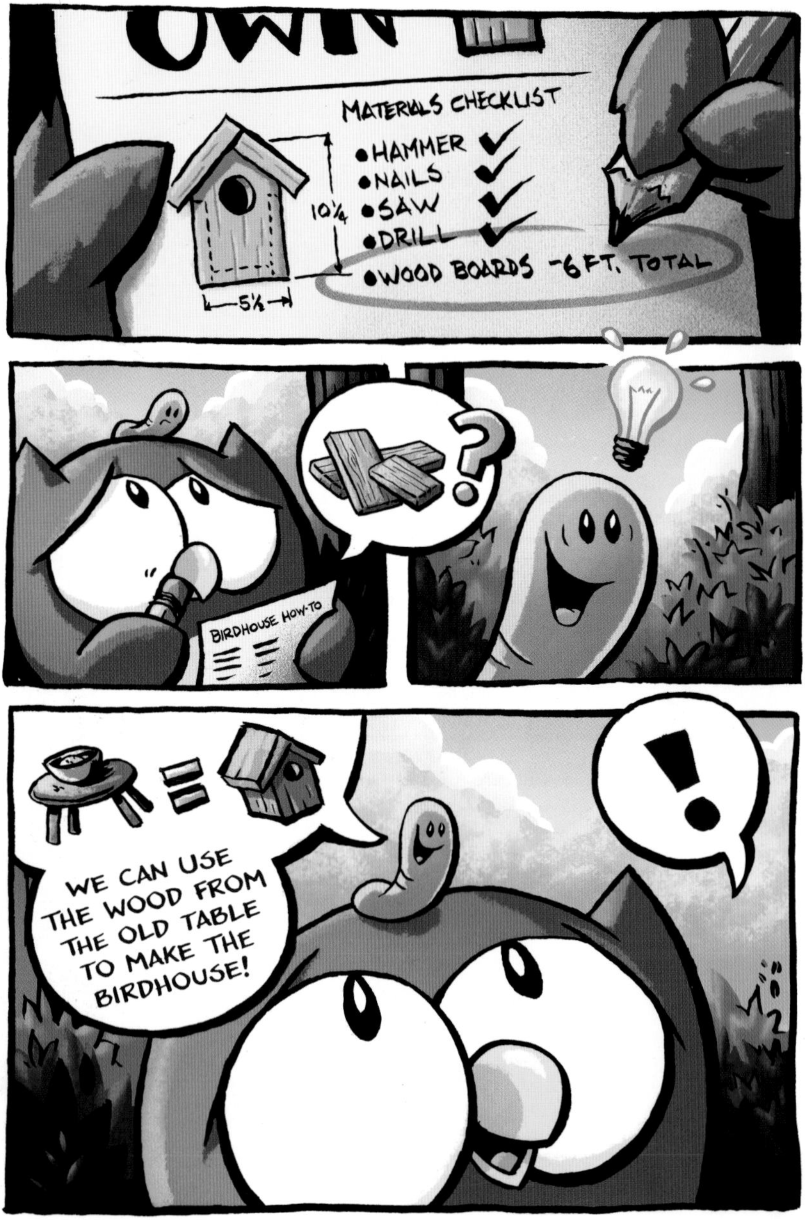
OWN
MATERIALS CHECKLIST
•HAMMER
•NAILS
•SAW
•DRILL
•WOOD BOARDS –6 FT. TOTAL
10¼
5½
BIRDHOUSE HOW-TO
?
WE CAN USE THE WOOD FROM THE OLD TABLE TO MAKE THE BIRDHOUSE!
!

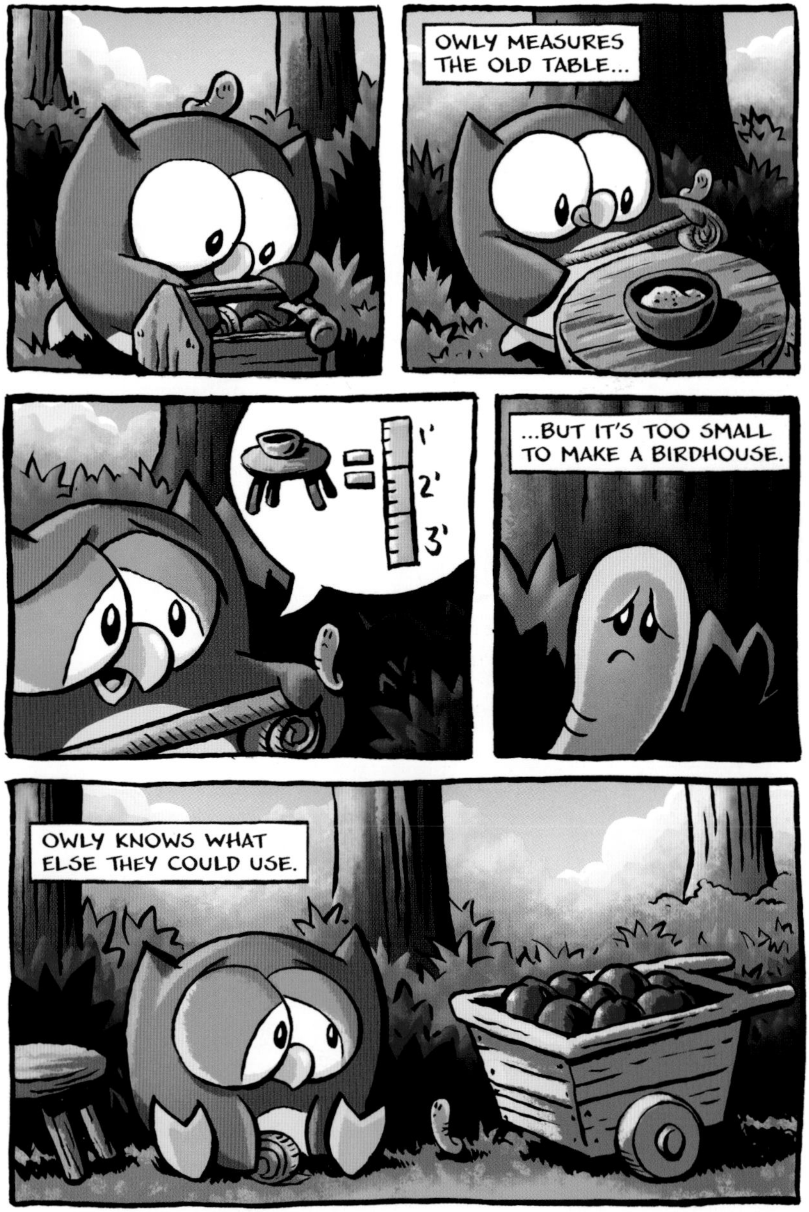
OWLY MEASURES THE OLD TABLE...
1'
2'
3'
...BUT IT'S TOO SMALL TO MAKE A BIRDHOUSE.
OWLY KNOWS WHAT ELSE THEY COULD USE.

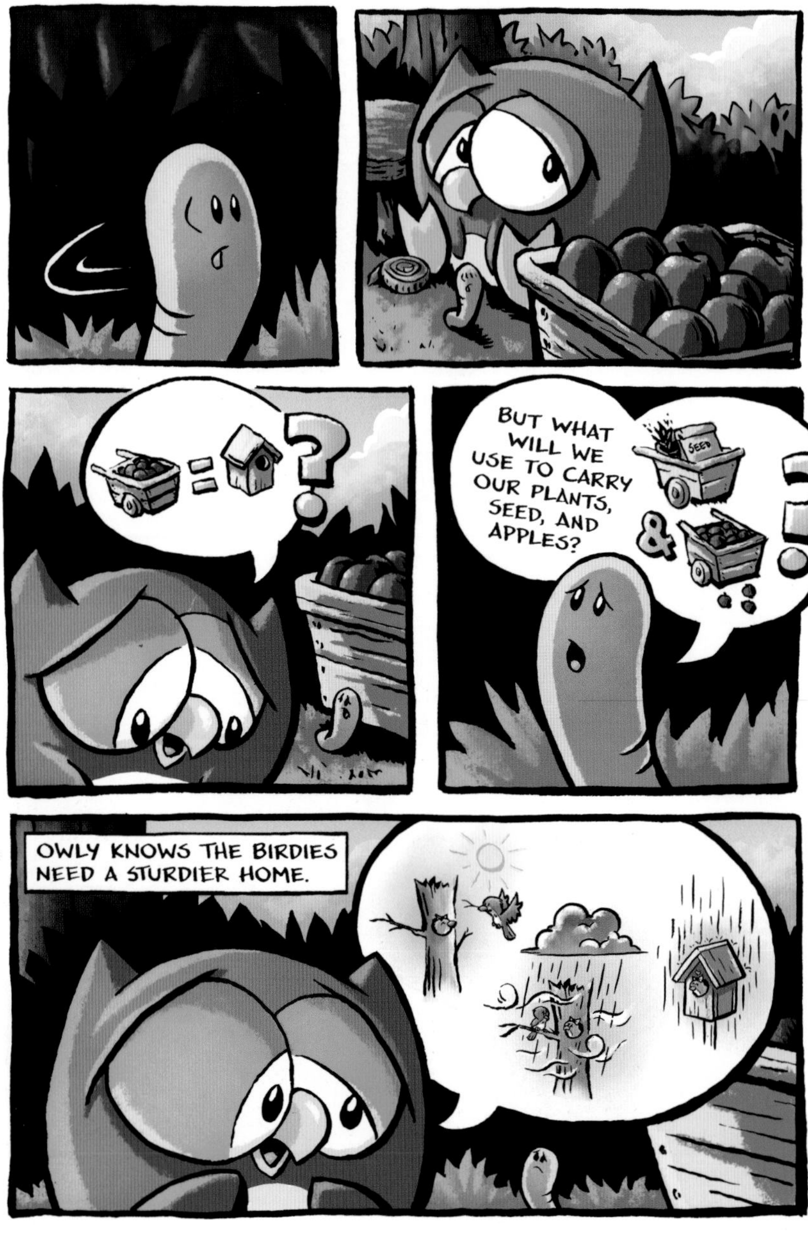
SEED
BUT WHAT WILL WE USE TO CARRY OUR PLANTS, SEED, AND APPLES?
OWLY KNOWS THE BIRDIES NEED A STURDIER HOME.

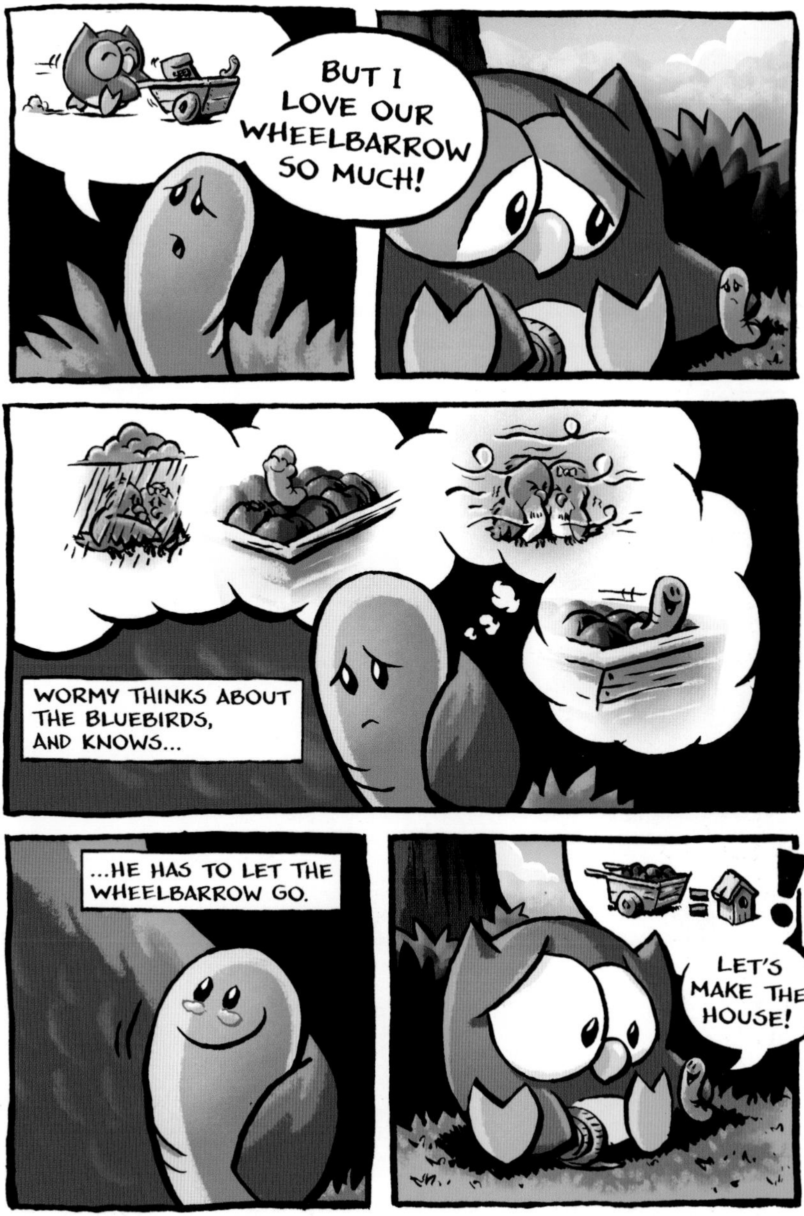
BUT I LOVE OUR WHEELBARROW SO MUCH!
WORMY THINKS ABOUT THE BLUEBIRDS, AND KNOWS...
...HE HAS TO LET THE WHEELBARROW GO.
LET'S MAKE THE HOUSE!

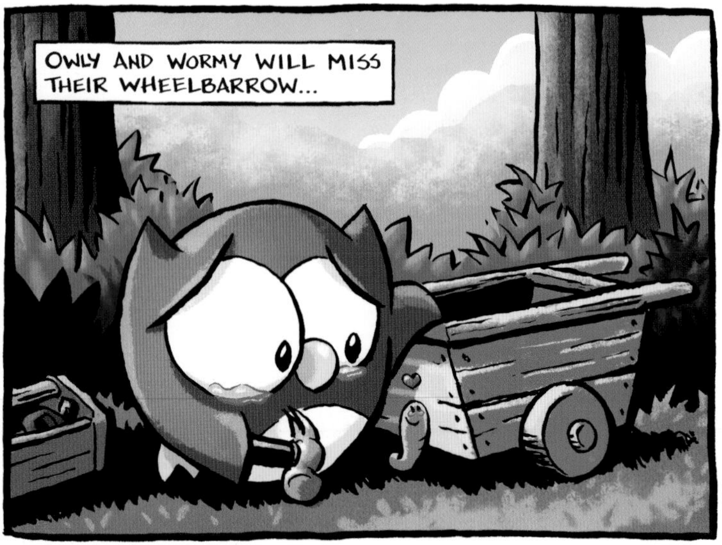
OWLY AND WORMY WILL MISS THEIR WHEELBARROW...

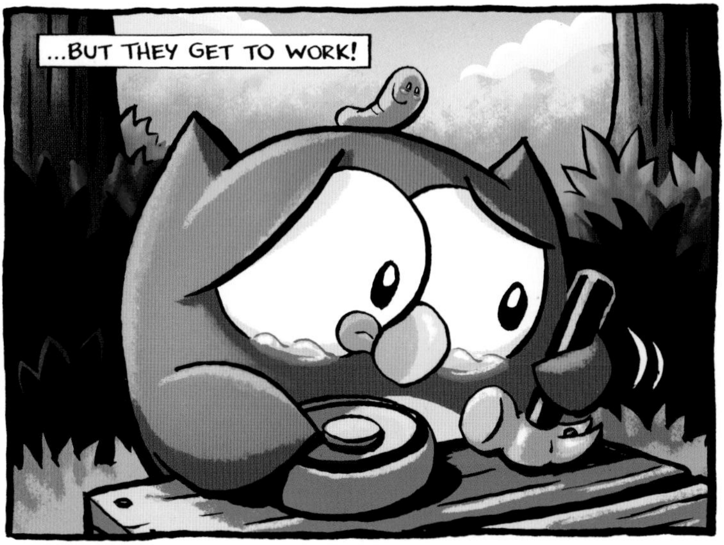
...BUT THEY GET TO WORK!

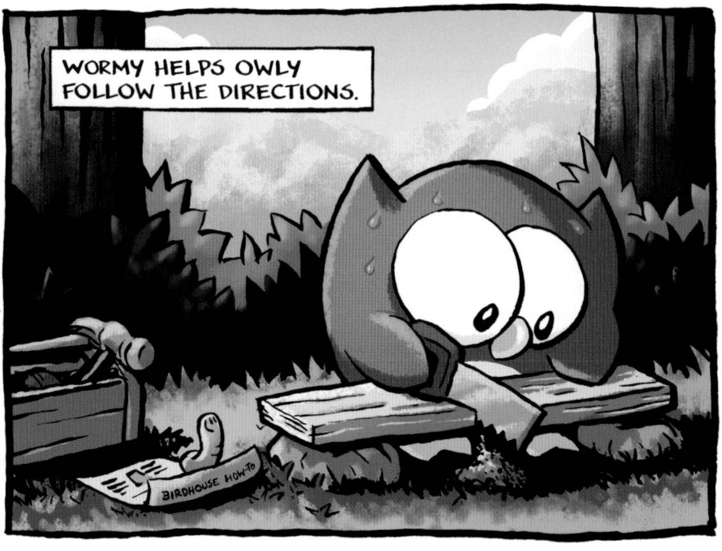
WORMY HELPS OWLY
FOLLOW THE DIRECTIONS.
BIRDHOUSE HOW-TO

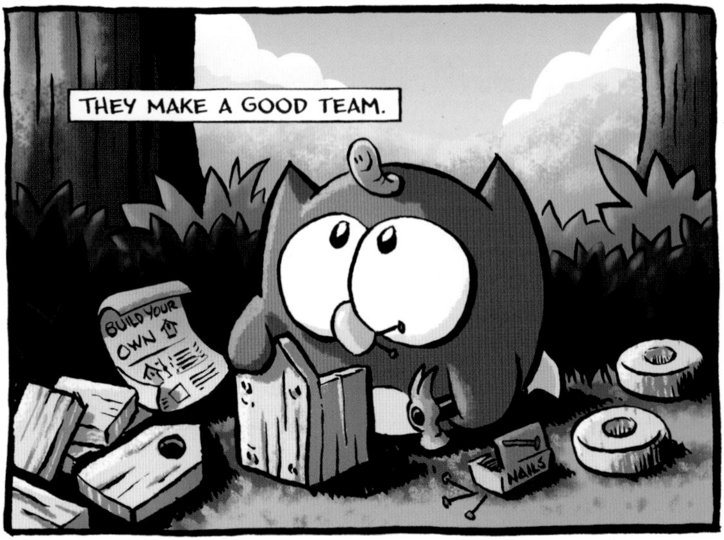
THEY MAKE A GOOD TEAM.
BUILD YOUR OWN
NAILS

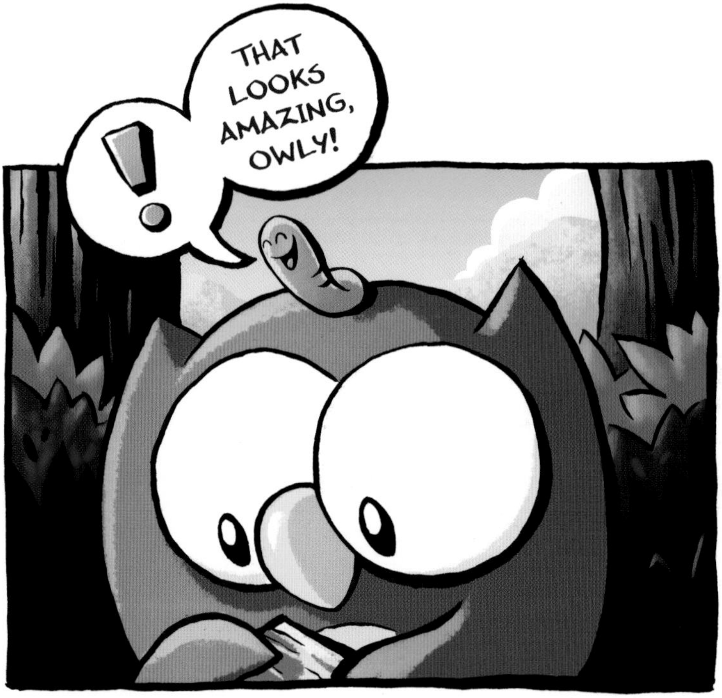
!
THAT LOOKS AMAZING, OWLY!

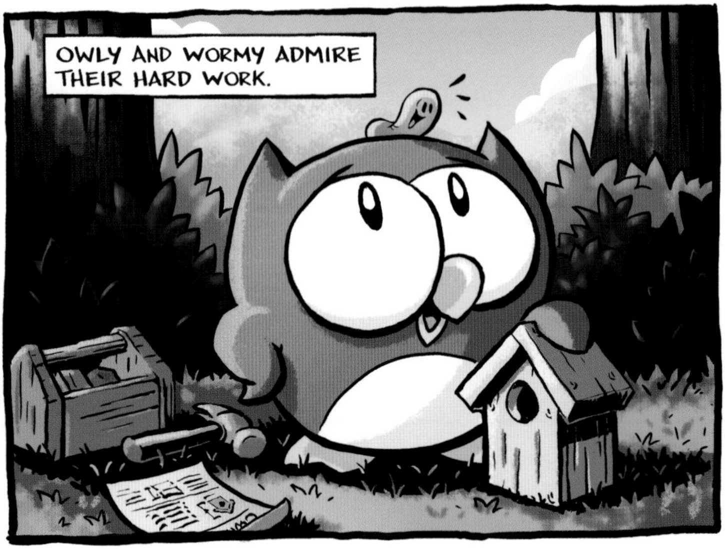
OWLY AND WORMY ADMIRE THEIR HARD WORK.

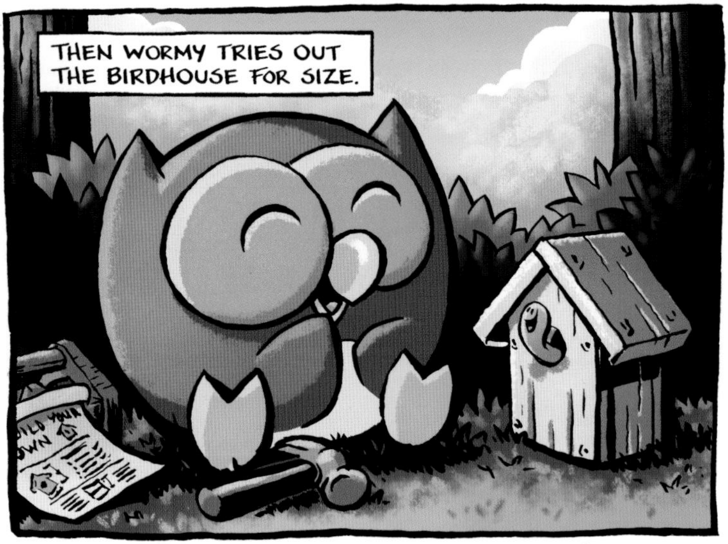
THEN WORMY TRIES OUT THE BIRDHOUSE FOR SIZE.
BUILD YOUR OWN

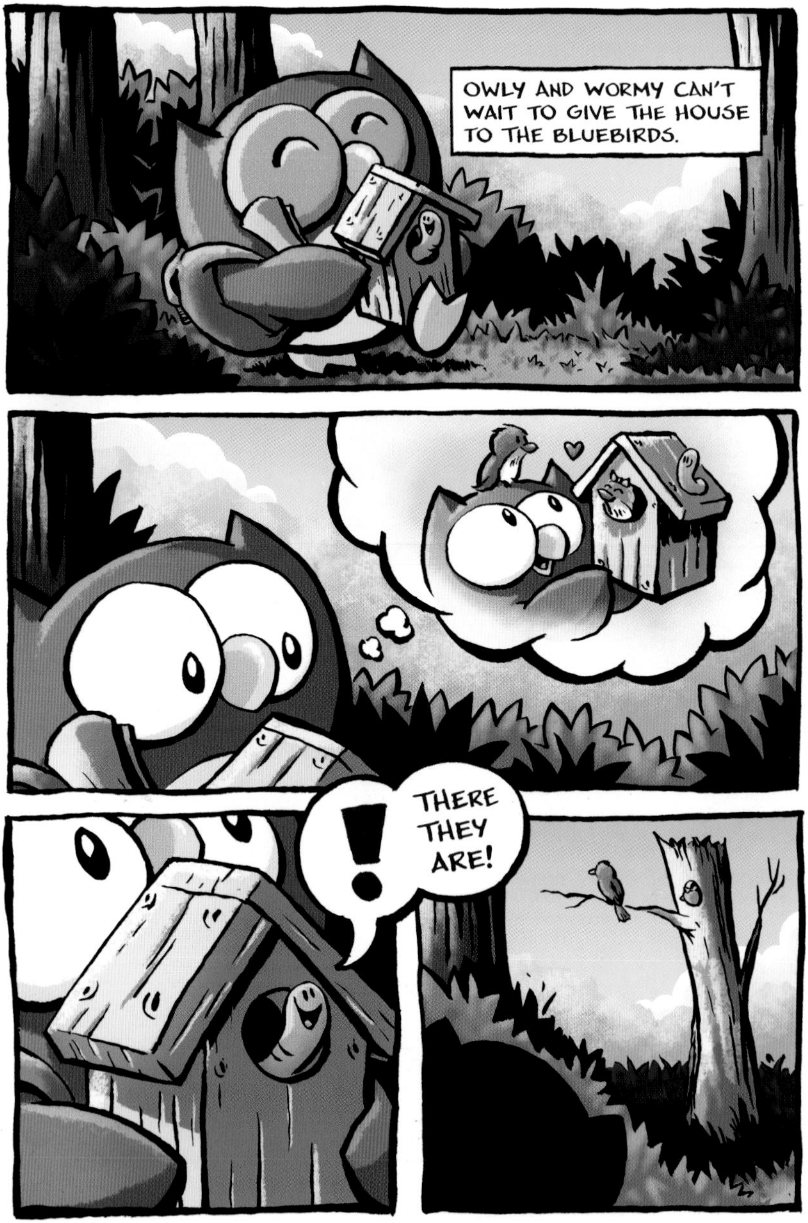
OWLY AND WORMY CAN'T WAIT TO GIVE THE HOUSE TO THE BLUEBIRDS.
!
THERE THEY ARE!

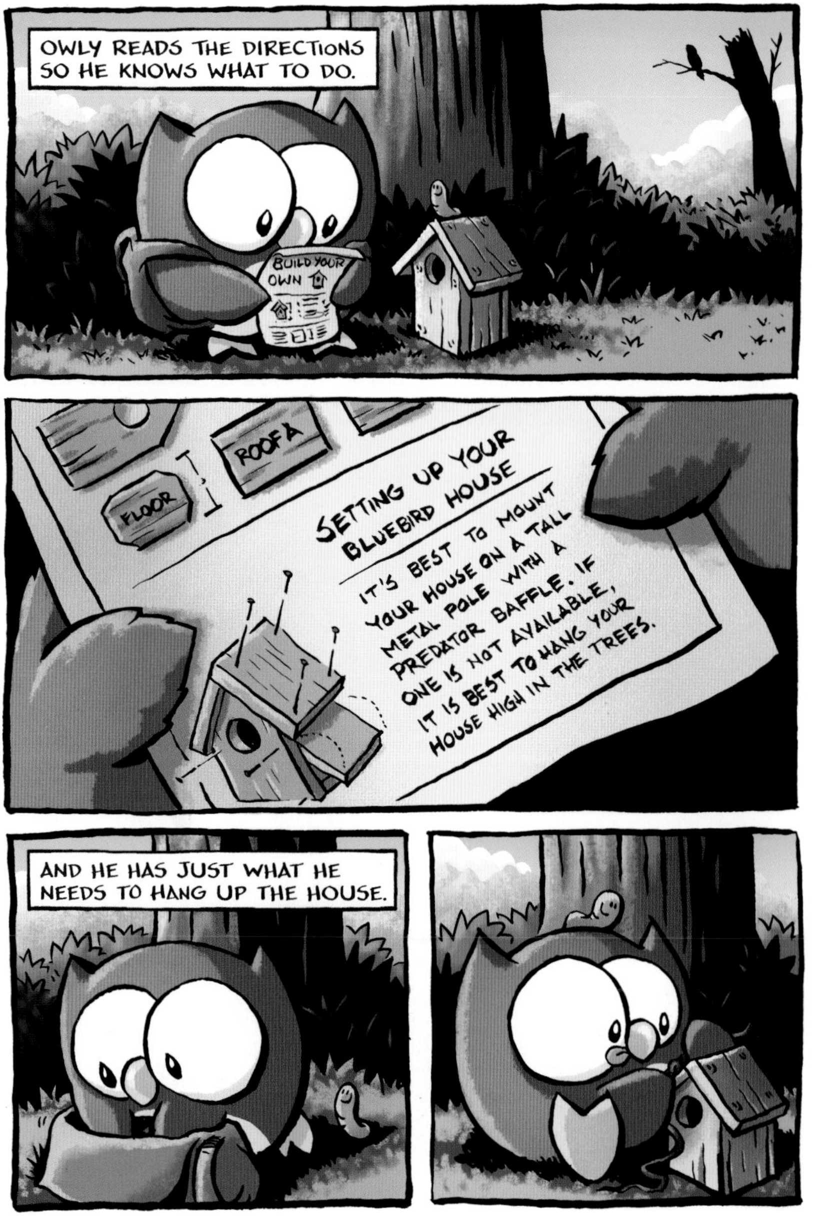
OWLY READS THE DIRECTIONS SO HE KNOWS WHAT TO DO.
BUILD YOUR OWN
ROOF A
FLOOR
SETTING UP YOUR BLUEBIRD HOUSE
IT'S BEST TO MOUNT YOUR HOUSE ON A TALL METAL POLE WITH A PREDATOR BAFFLE. IF ONE IS NOT AVAILABLE, IT IS BEST TO HANG YOUR HOUSE HIGH IN THE TREES.
AND HE HAS JUST WHAT HE NEEDS TO HANG UP THE HOUSE.

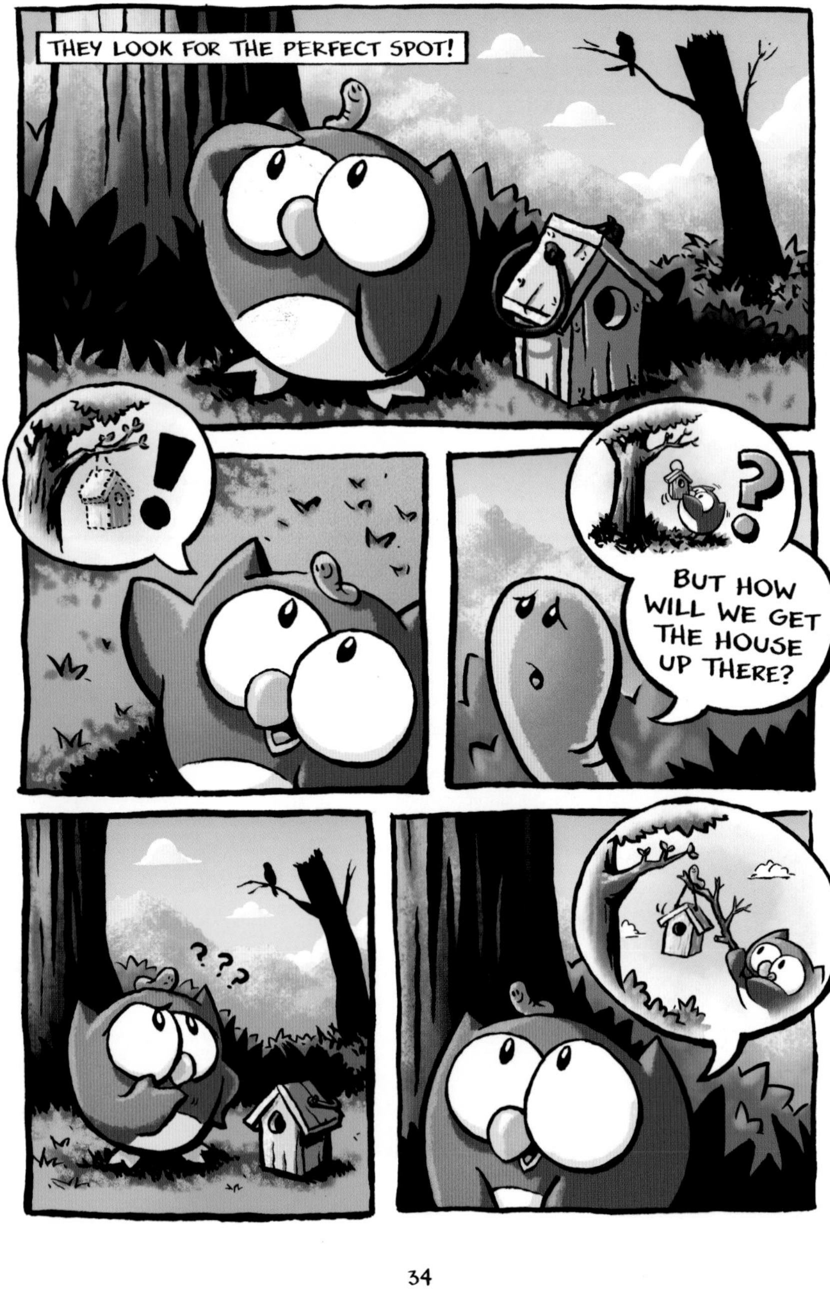
THEY LOOK FOR THE PERFECT SPOT!
!
?
BUT HOW WILL WE GET THE HOUSE UP THERE?
???

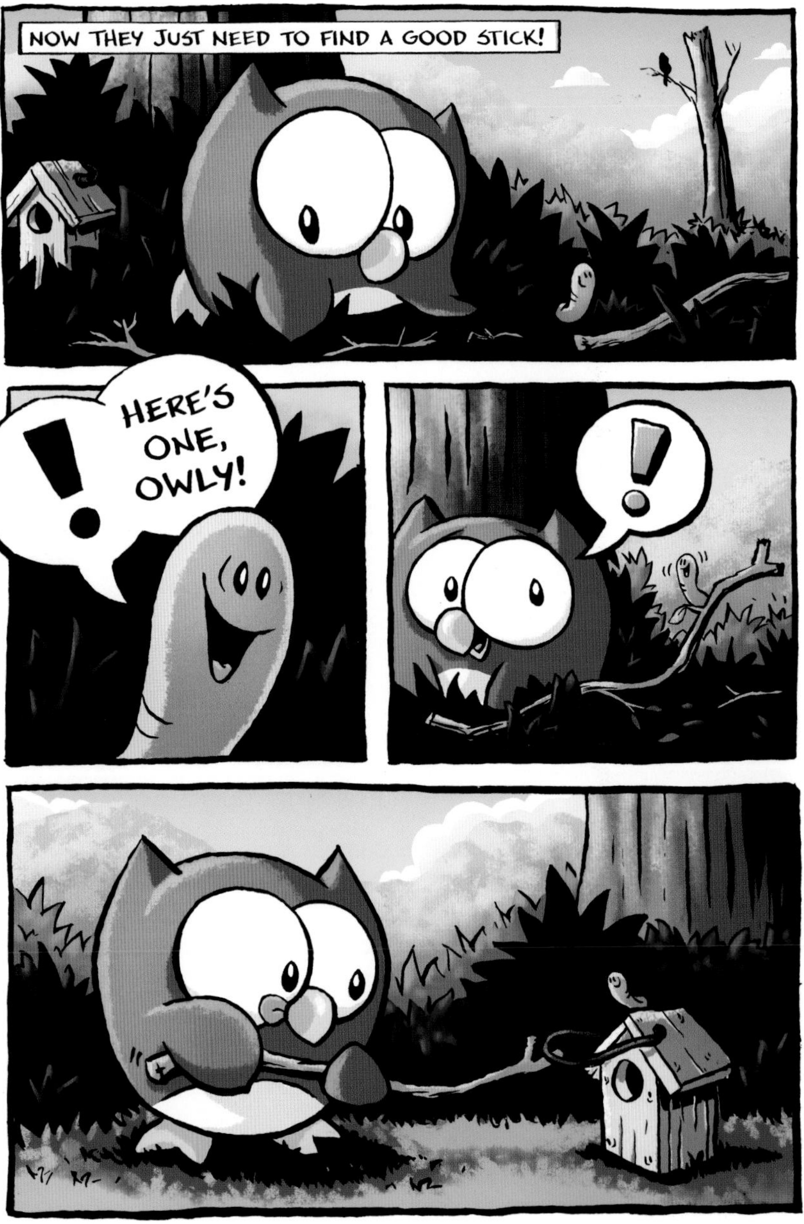
NOW THEY JUST NEED TO FIND A GOOD STICK!
! HERE'S ONE, OWLY!
!

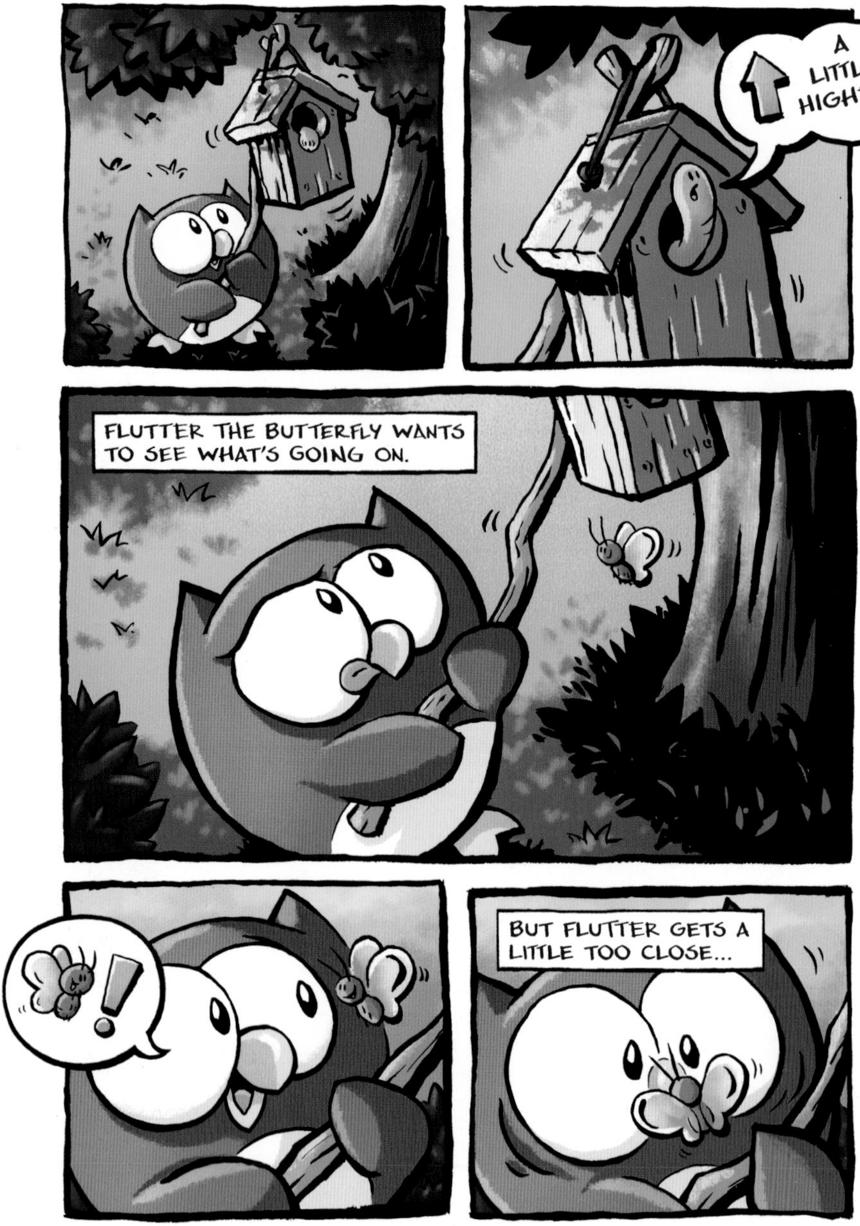
A LITTLE HIGHER.
FLUTTER THE BUTTERFLY WANTS TO SEE WHAT'S GOING ON.
!
BUT FLUTTER GETS A LITTLE TOO CLOSE...

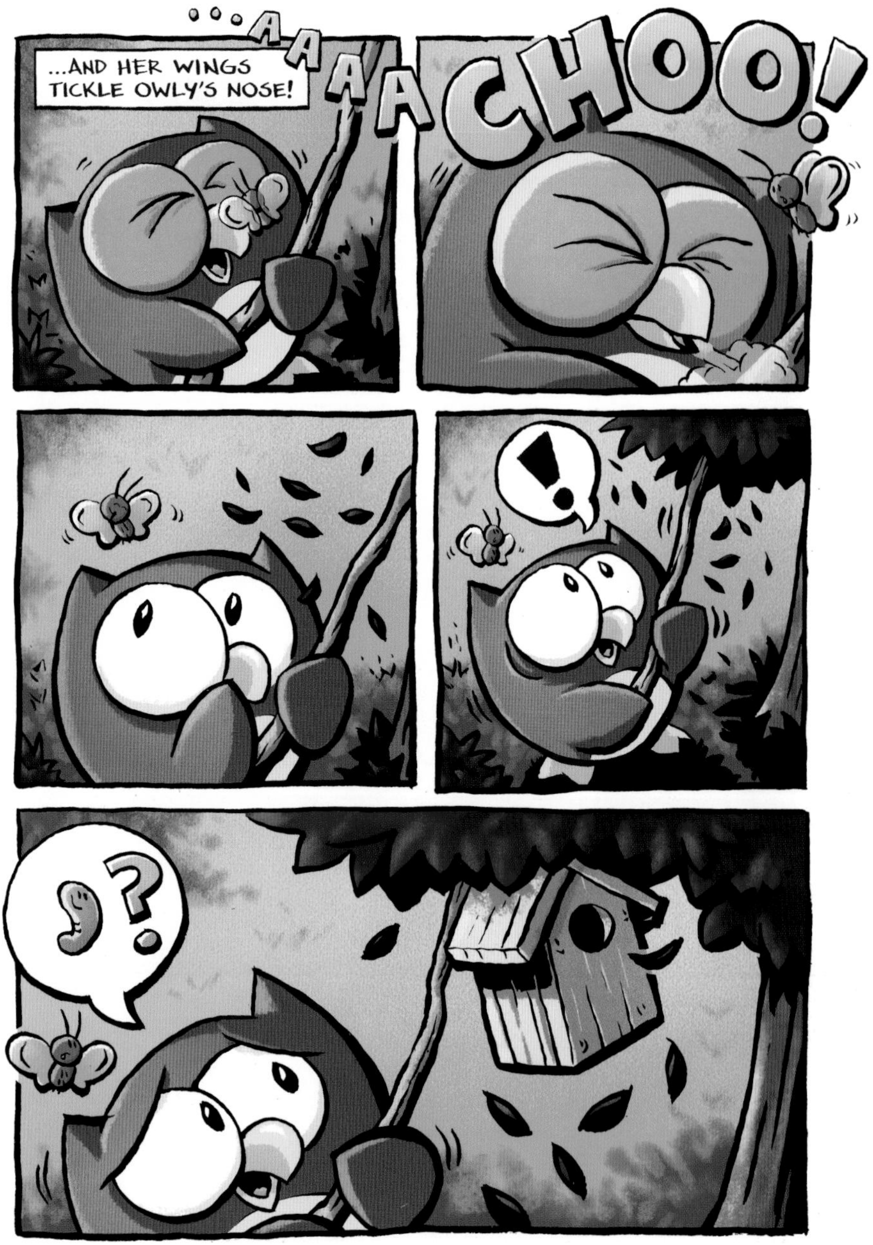
...AND HER WINGS TICKLE OWLY'S NOSE!
...AAAACHOO!
!
?

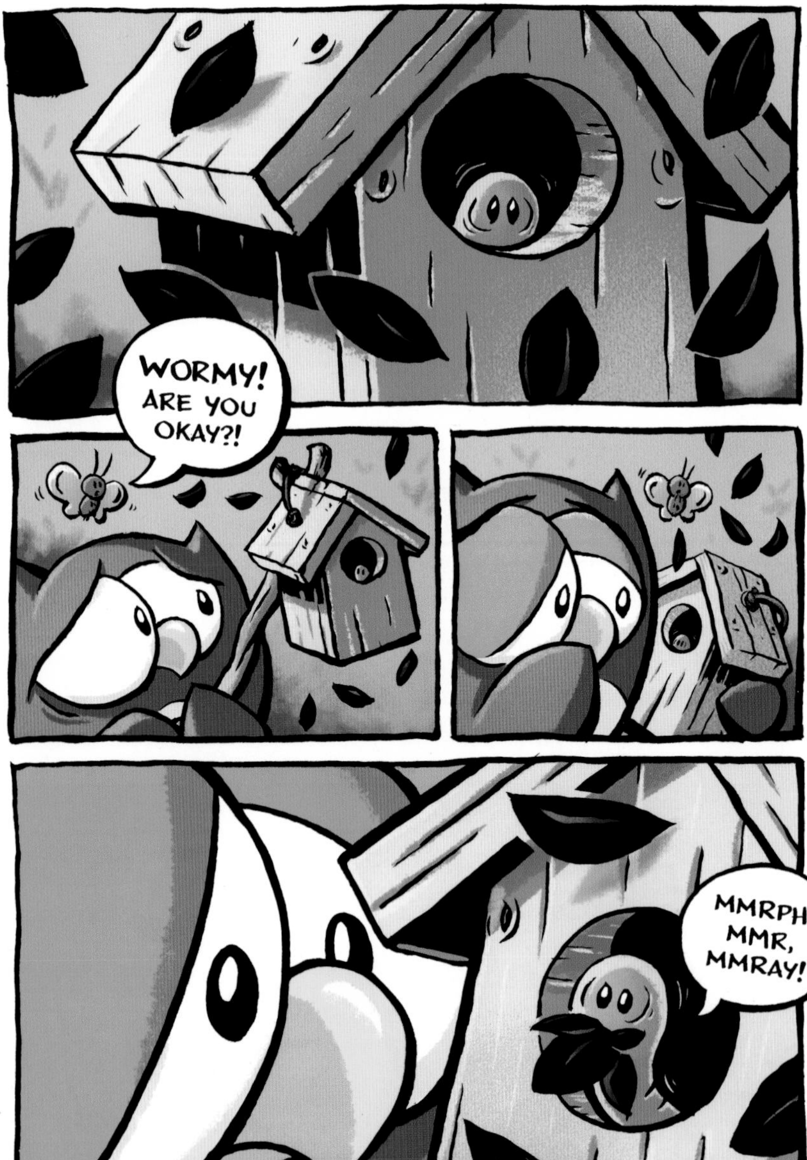
WORMY! ARE YOU OKAY?!
MMRPH, MMR, MMRAY!

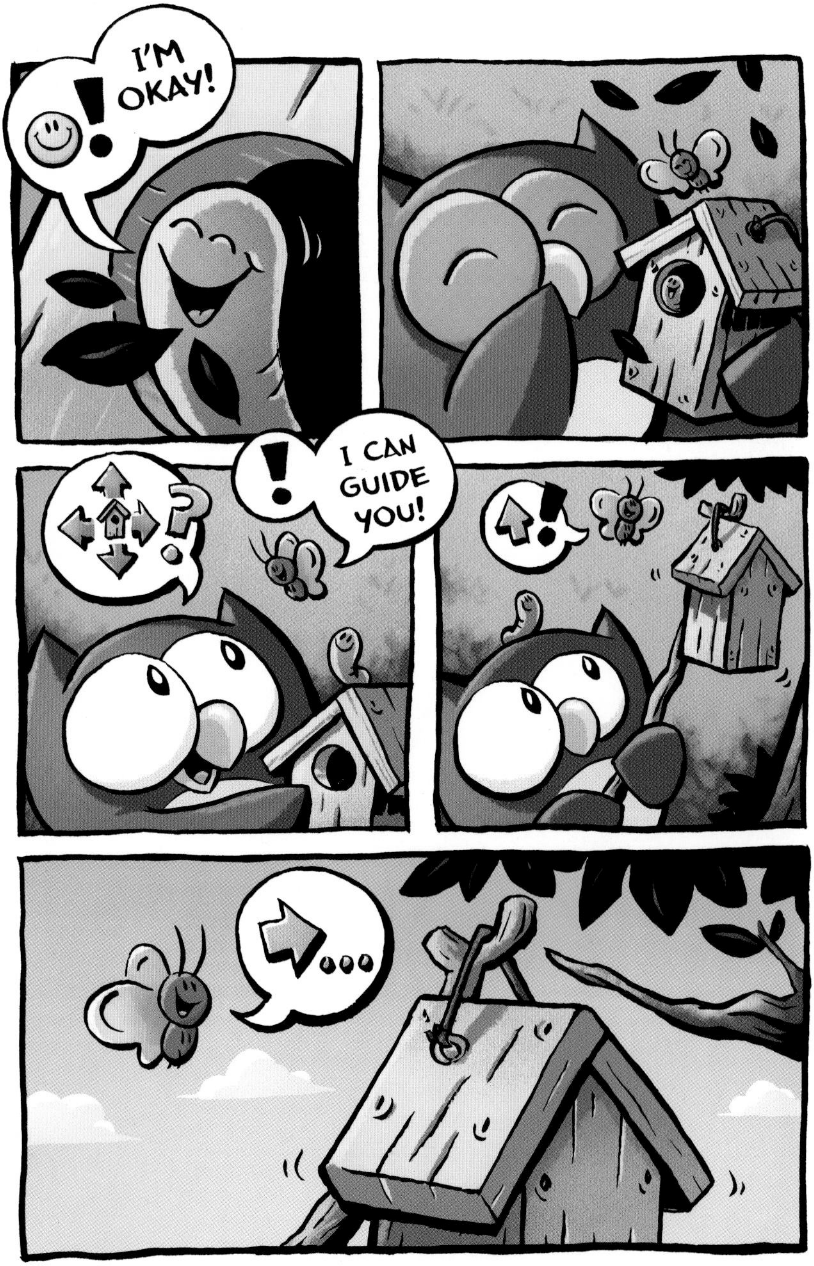
I'M OKAY!
I CAN GUIDE YOU!

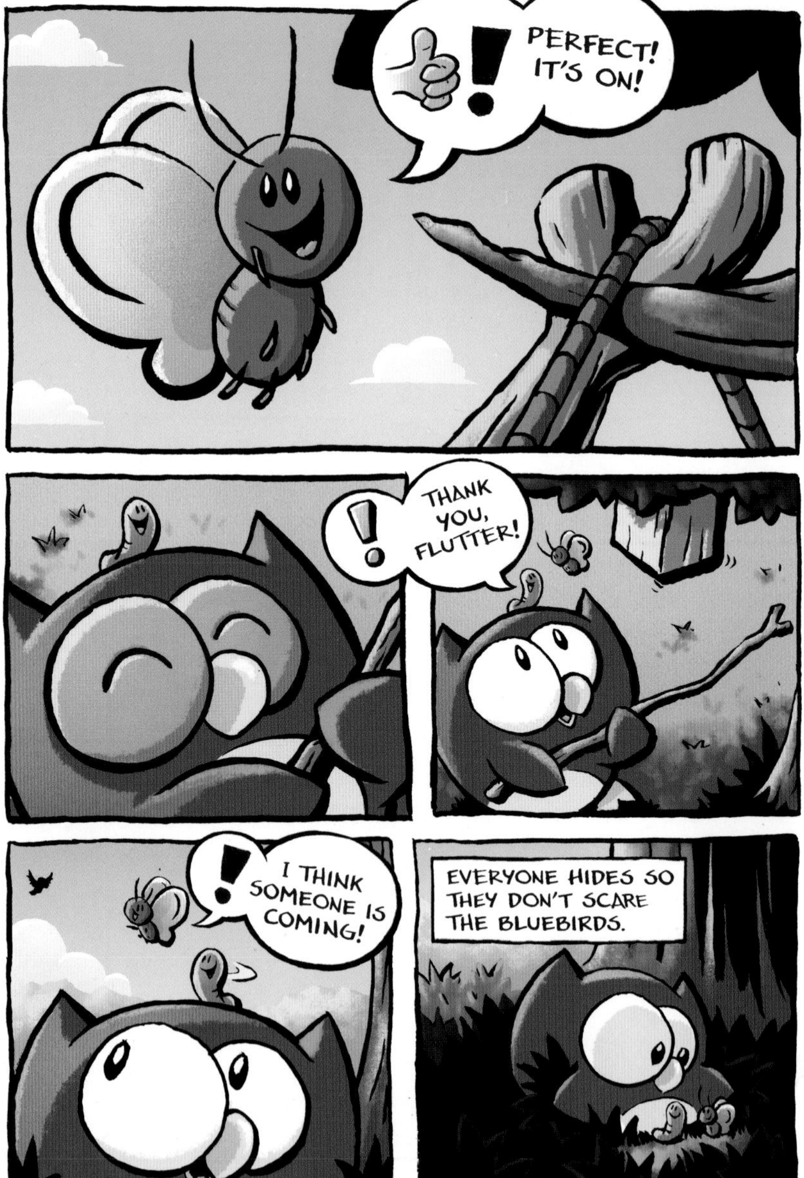
PERFECT! IT'S ON!
THANK YOU, FLUTTER!
I THINK SOMEONE IS COMING!
EVERYONE HIDES SO THEY DON'T SCARE THE BLUEBIRDS.

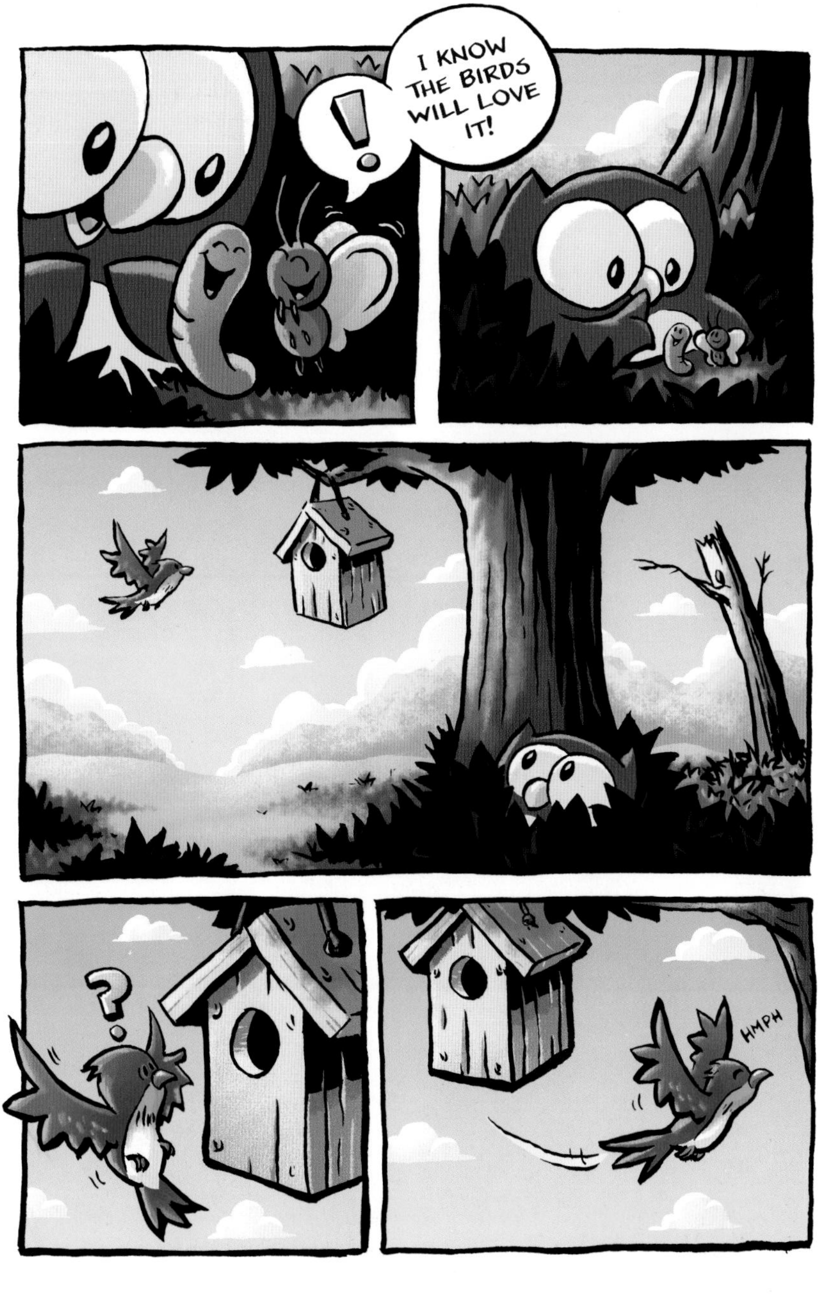
!
I KNOW THE BIRDS WILL LOVE IT!
?
HMPH

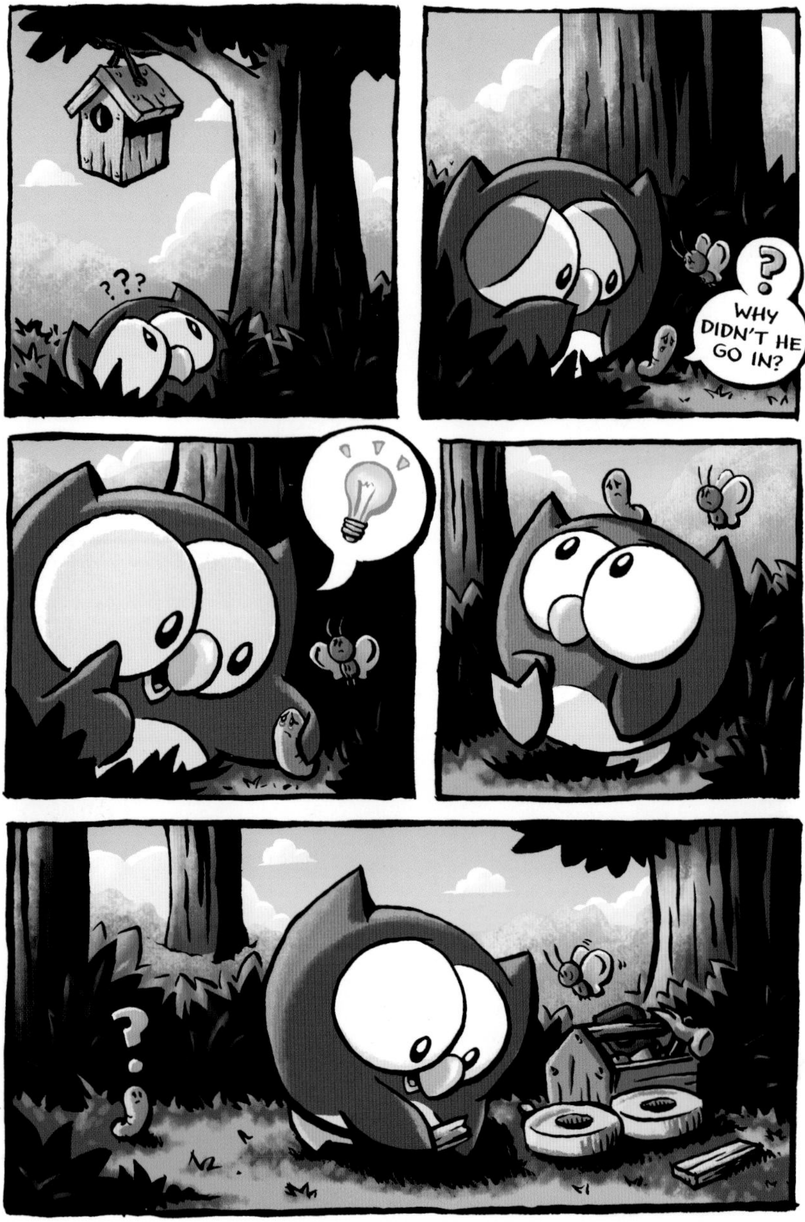
???
?
WHY DIDN'T HE GO IN?
?

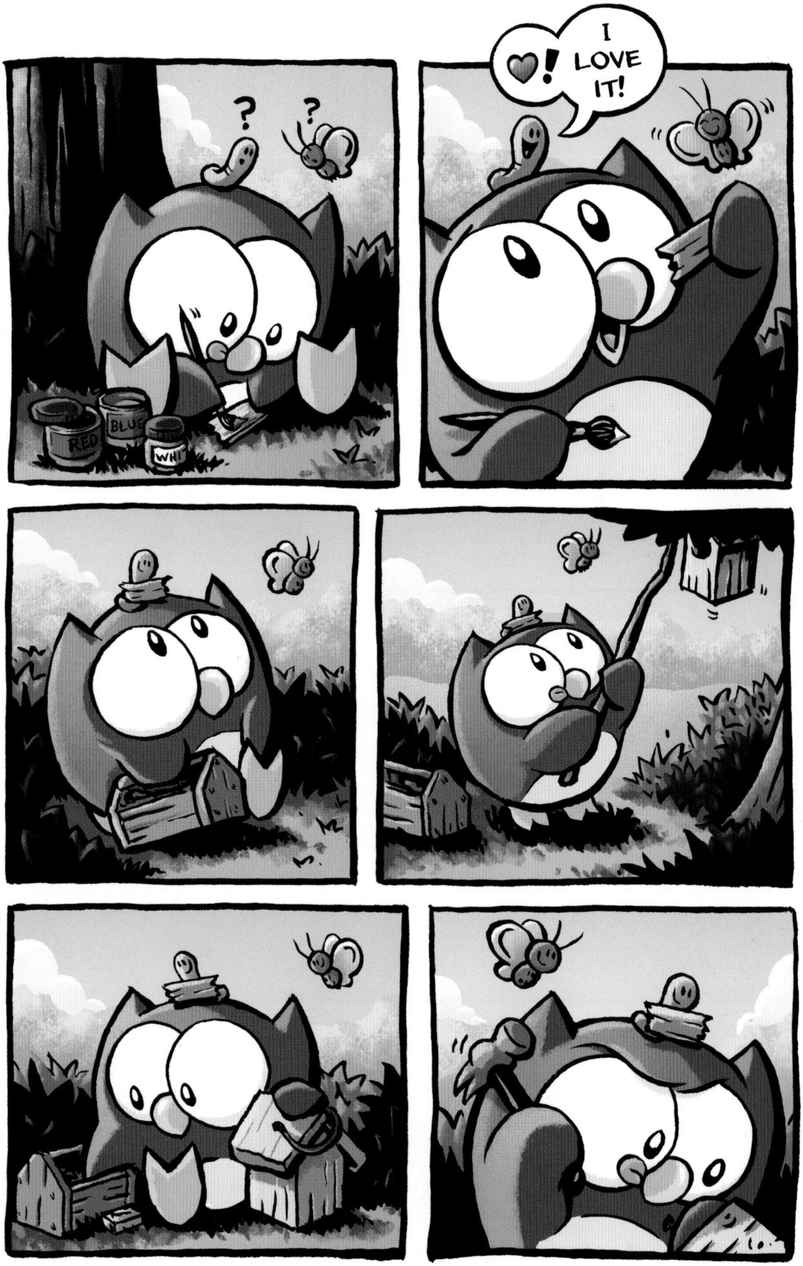
?
?
RED
BLUE
!
I LOVE IT!

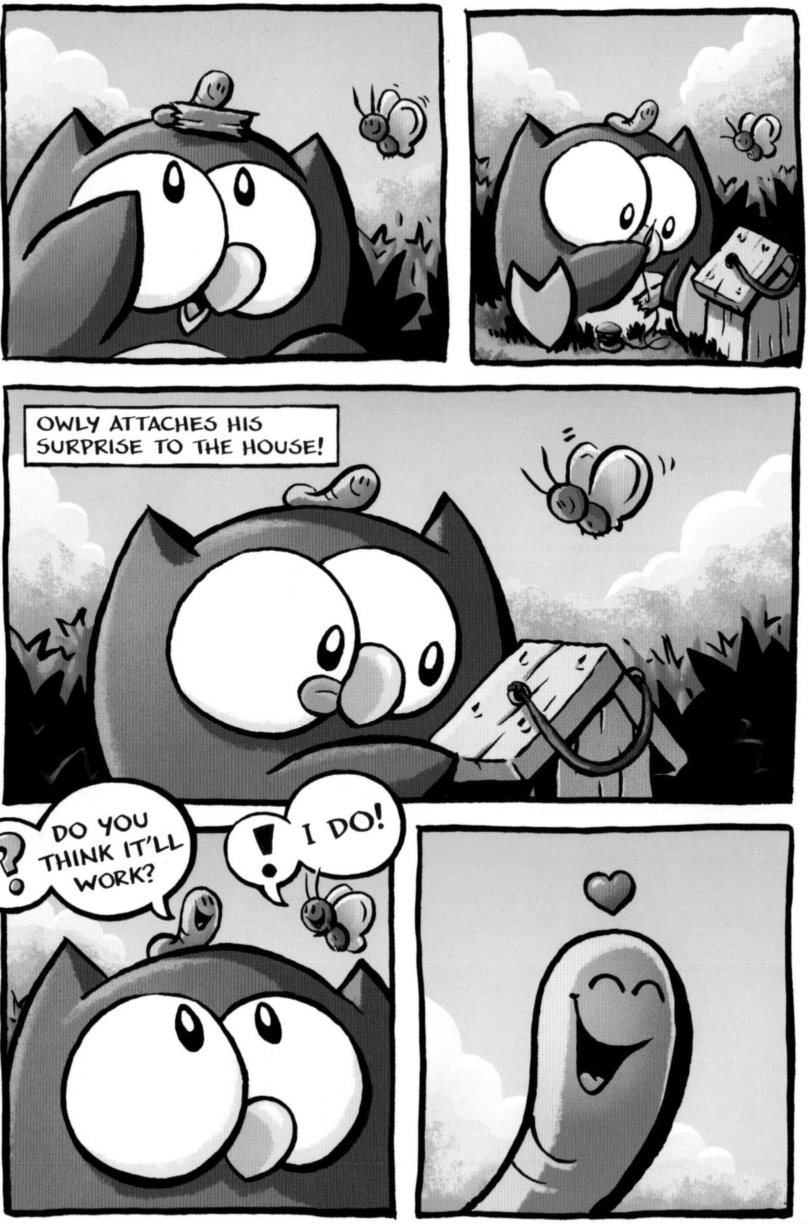
OWLY ATTACHES HIS SURPRISE TO THE HOUSE!
DO YOU THINK IT'LL WORK?
I DO!

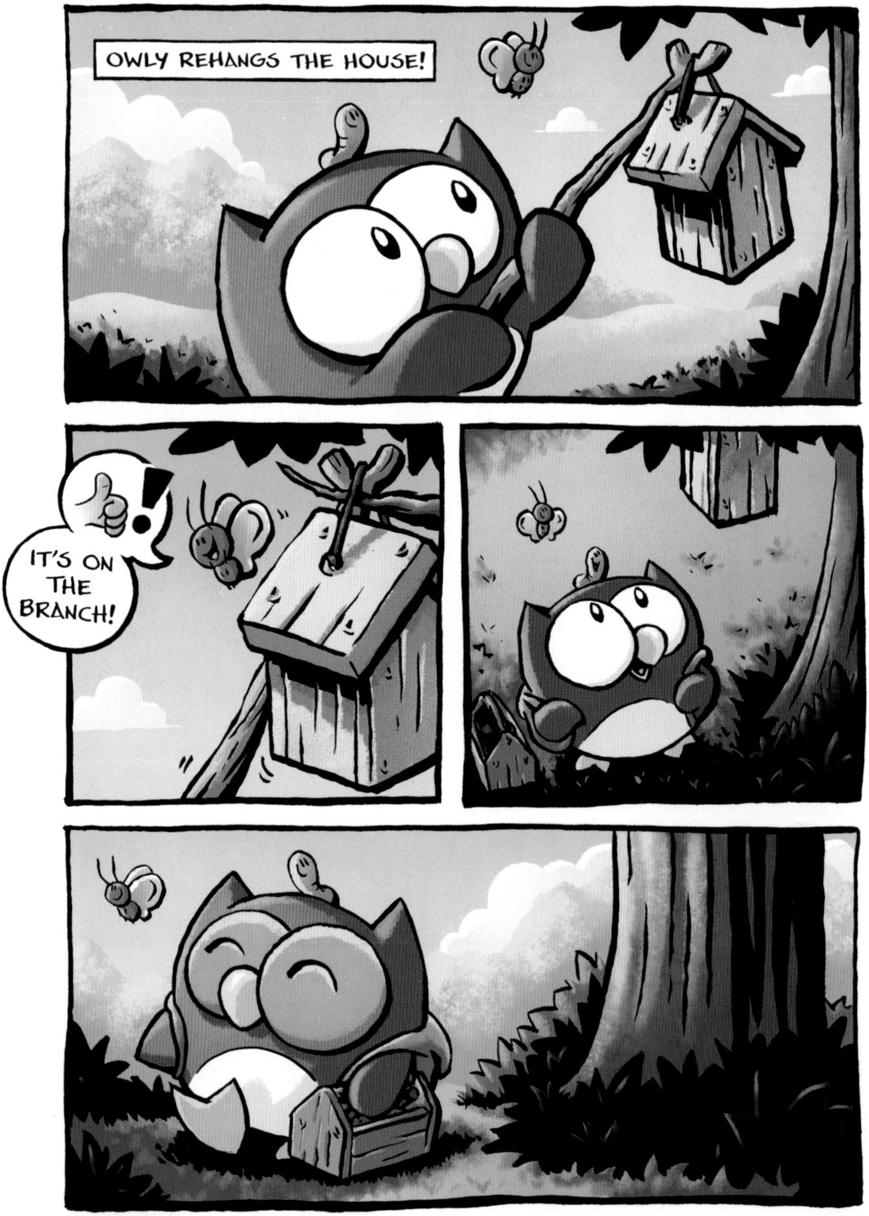
OWLY REHANGS THE HOUSE!
!
IT'S ON THE BRANCH!

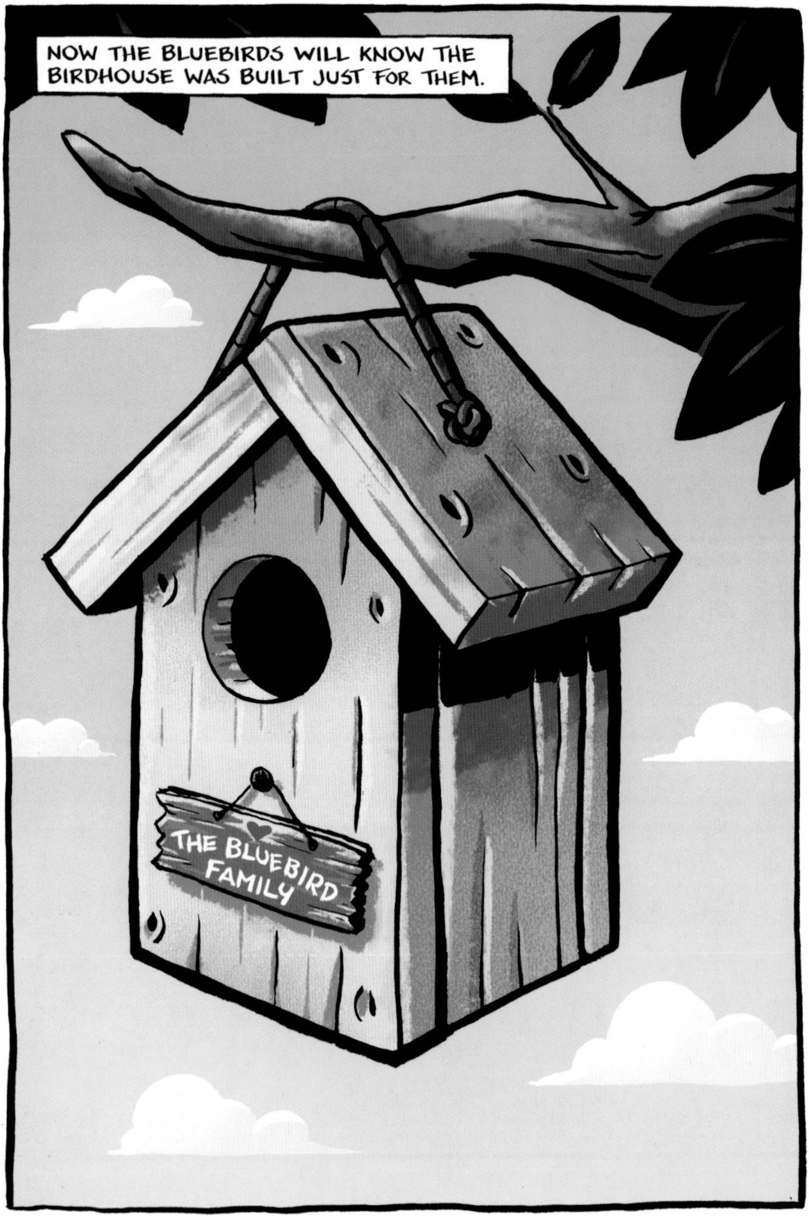
NOW THE BLUEBIRDS WILL KNOW THE BIRDHOUSE WAS BUILT JUST FOR THEM.
THE BLUEBIRD FAMILY

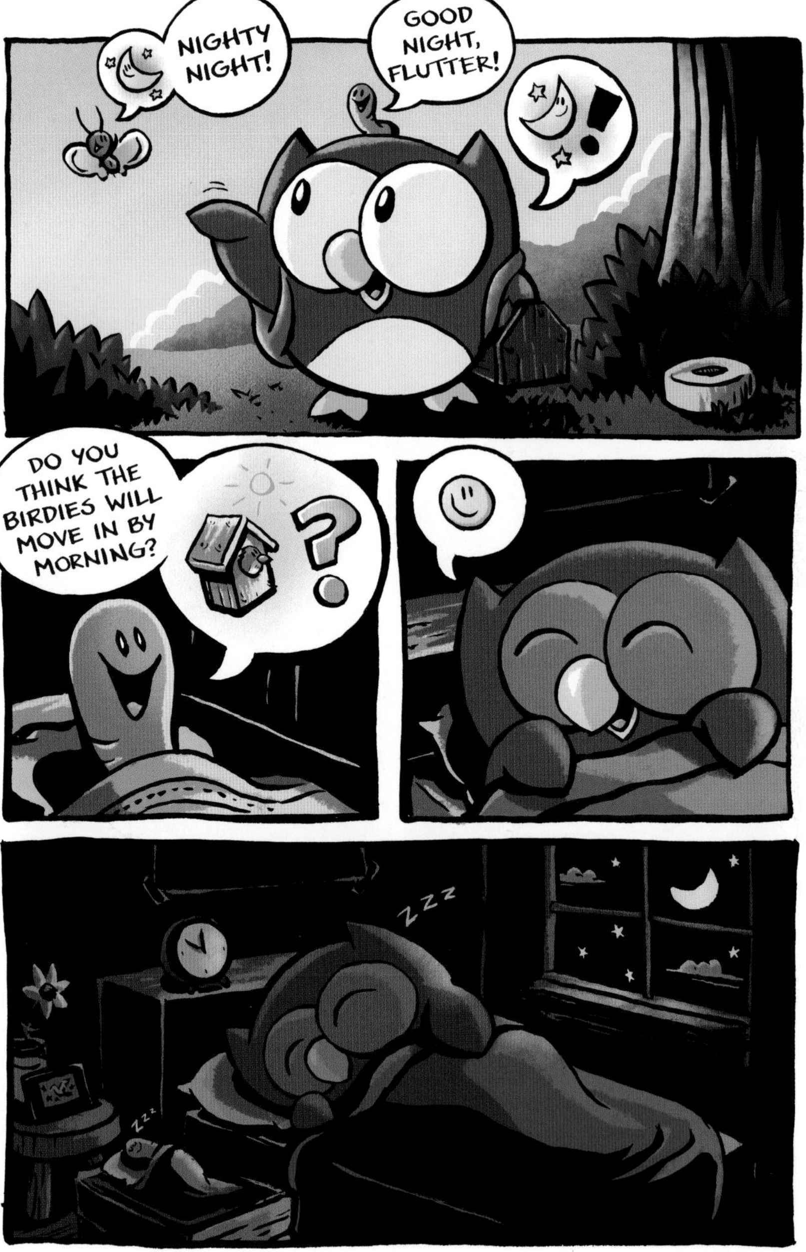
NIGHTY NIGHT!
GOOD NIGHT, FLUTTER!
DO YOU THINK THE BIRDIES WILL MOVE IN BY MORNING?
Z Z Z
Z Z Z

TICK TICK

TICK
TICK
TICK

?

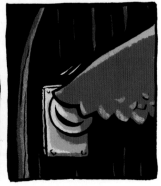

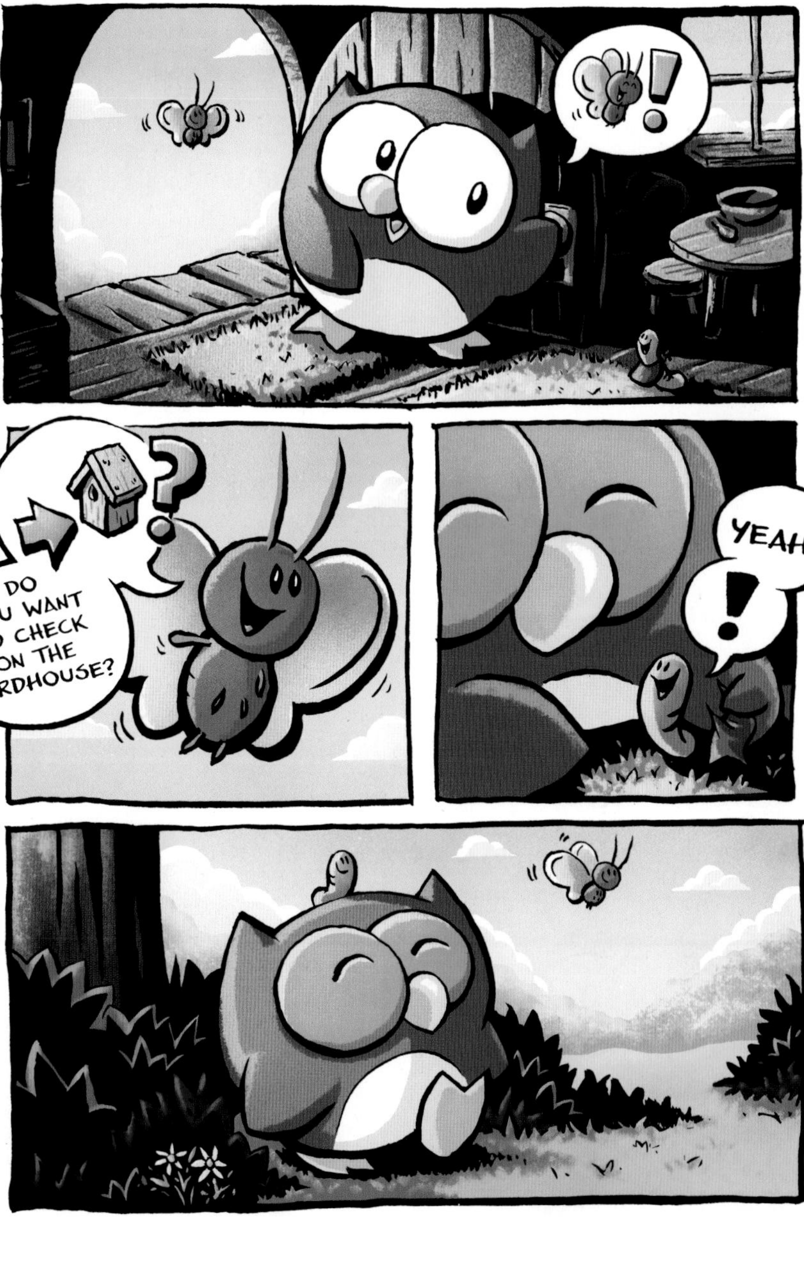
!
?
DO YOU WANT TO CHECK ON THE BIRDHOUSE?
YEAH!
!

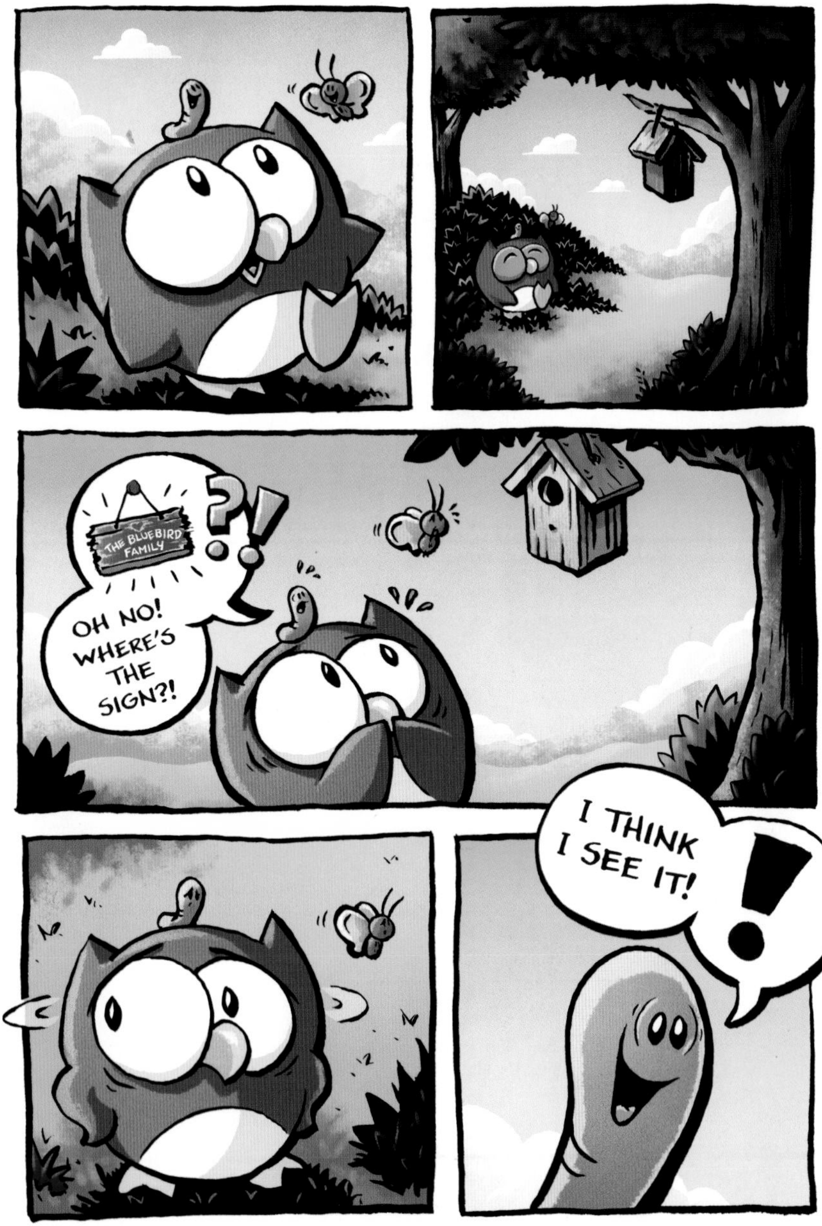
THE BLUEBIRD FAMILY
?!
OH NO! WHERE'S THE SIGN?!
I THINK I SEE IT!
!

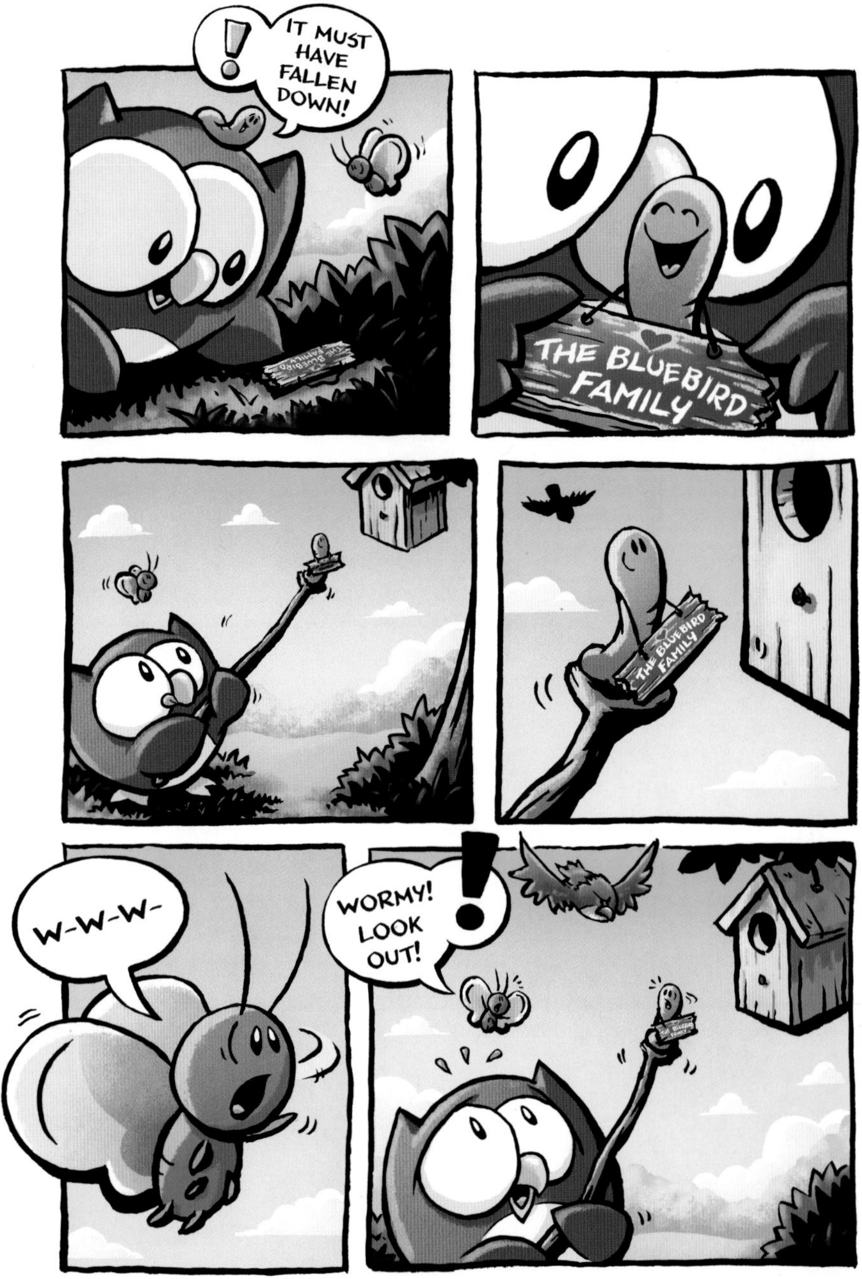
!
IT MUST HAVE FALLEN DOWN!
THE BLUEBIRD FAMILY
THE BLUEBIRD FAMILY
W-W-W-
WORMY! LOOK OUT!
!

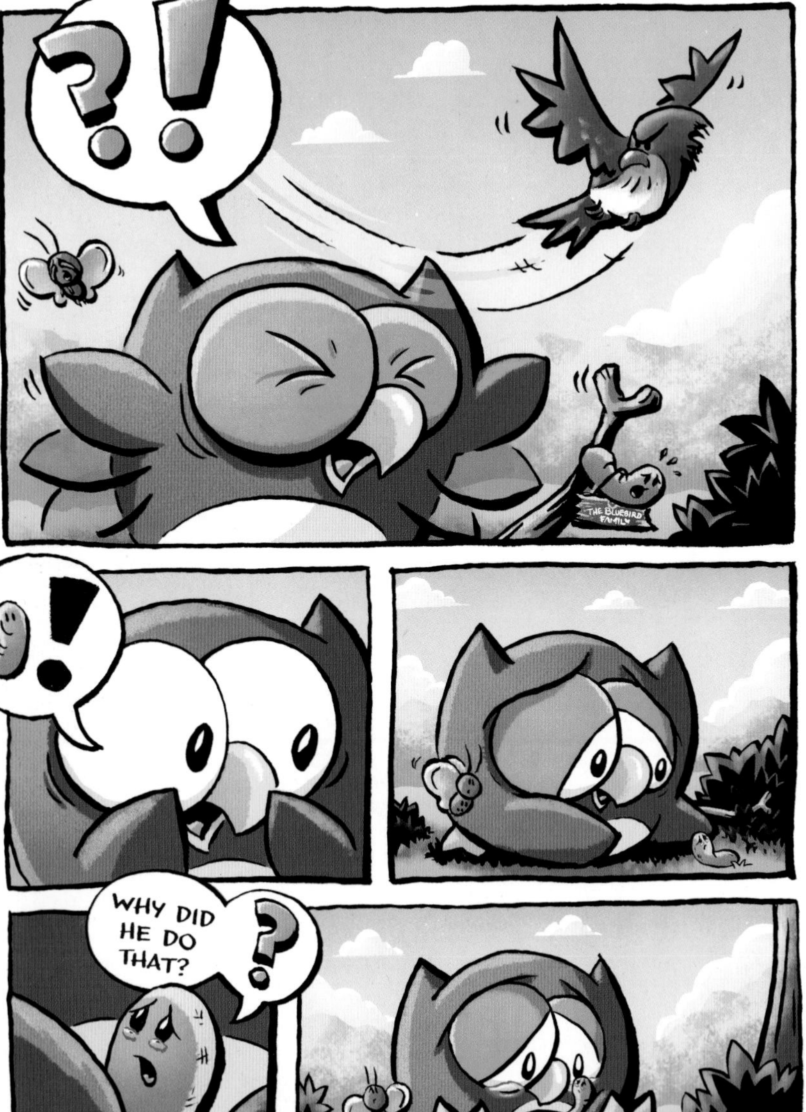
?!
THE BLUEBIRD FAMILY
!
WHY DID HE DO THAT?
?

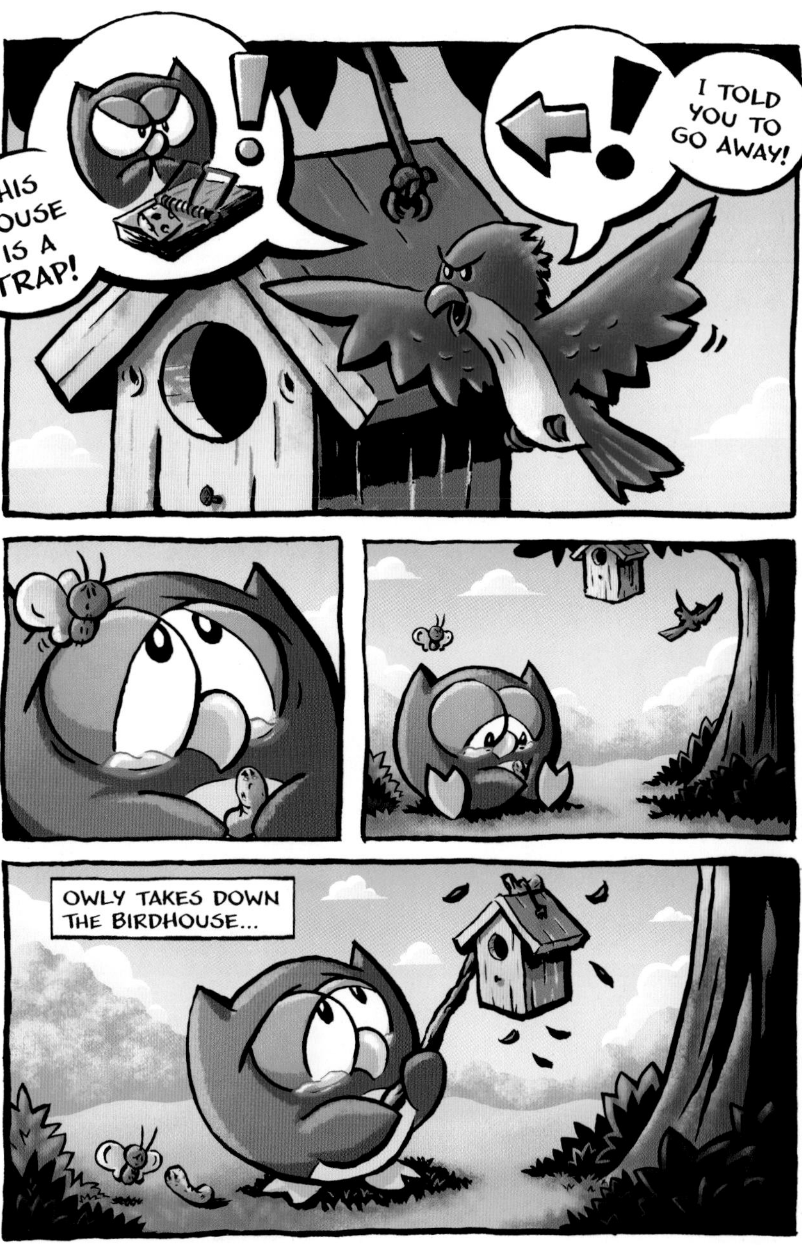
THIS HOUSE IS A TRAP!
I TOLD YOU TO GO AWAY!
OWLY TAKES DOWN THE BIRDHOUSE...

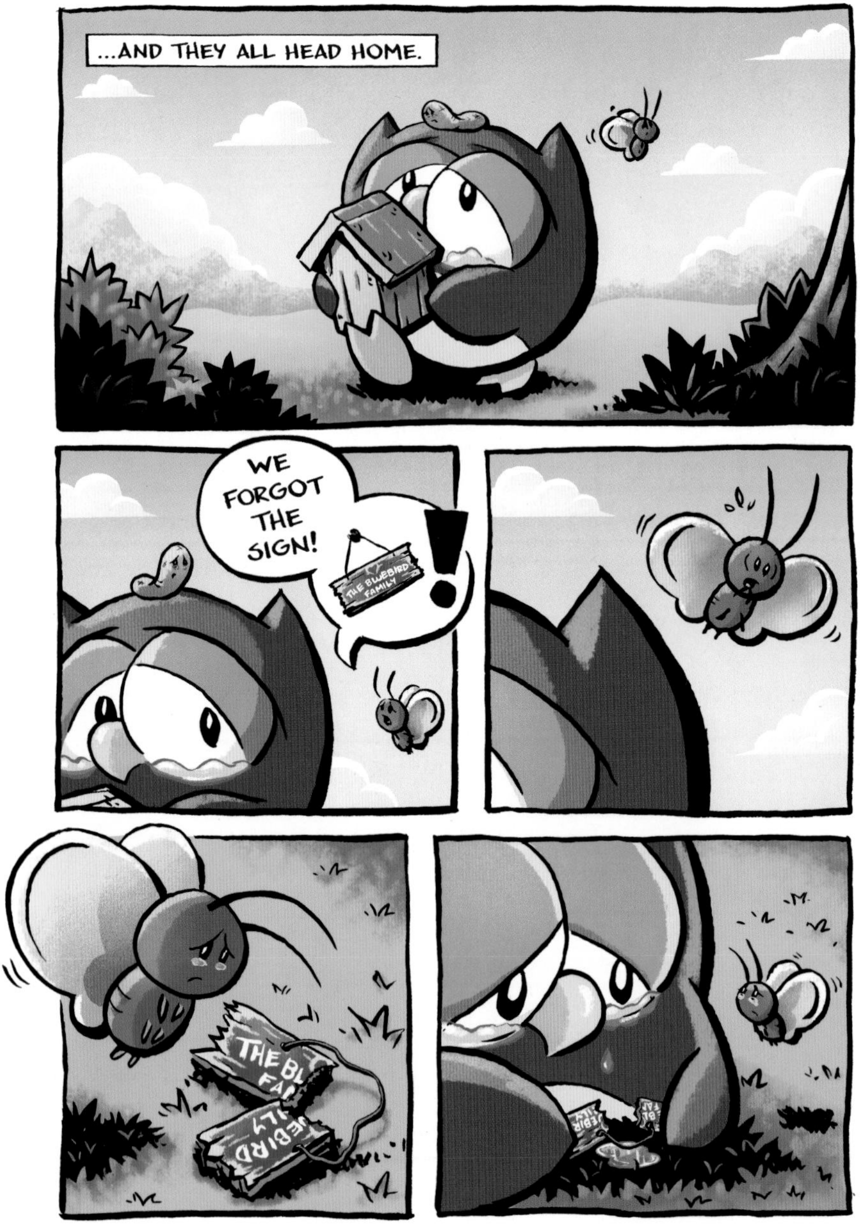
...AND THEY ALL HEAD HOME.
WE FORGOT THE SIGN!
THE BLUEBIRD FAMILY

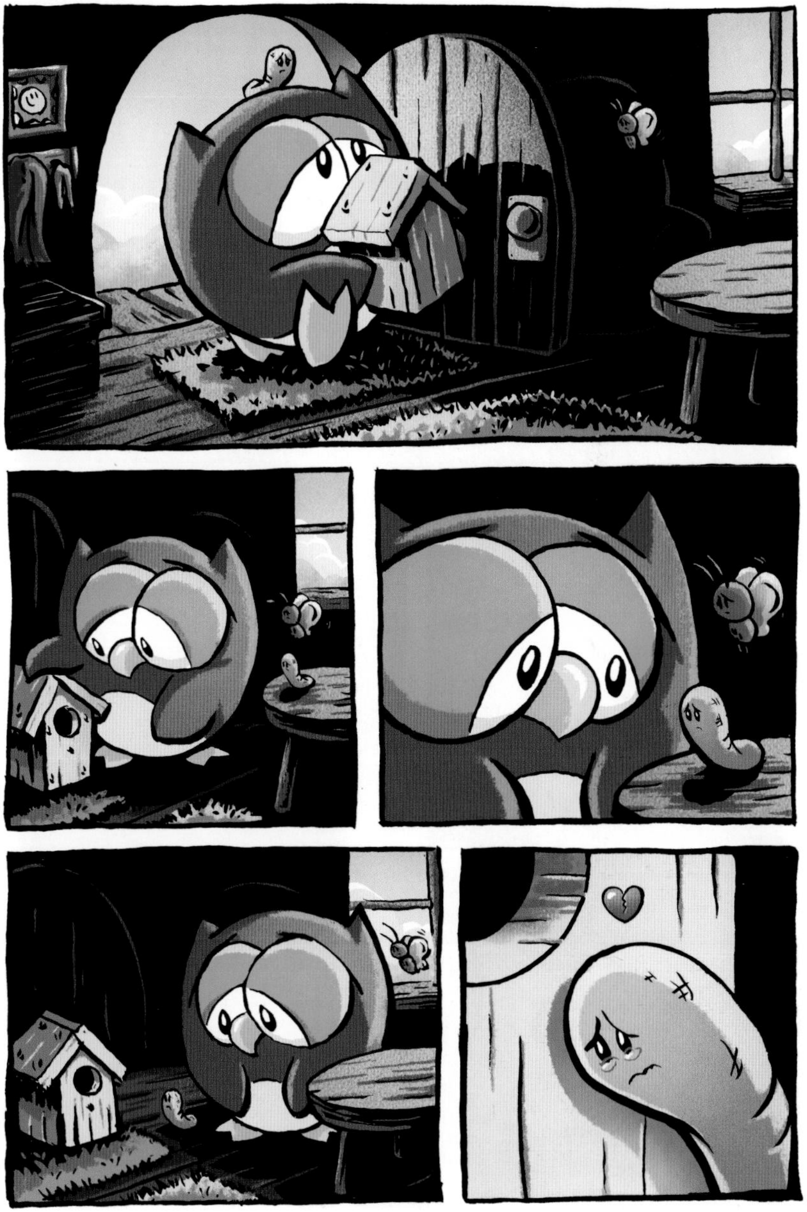

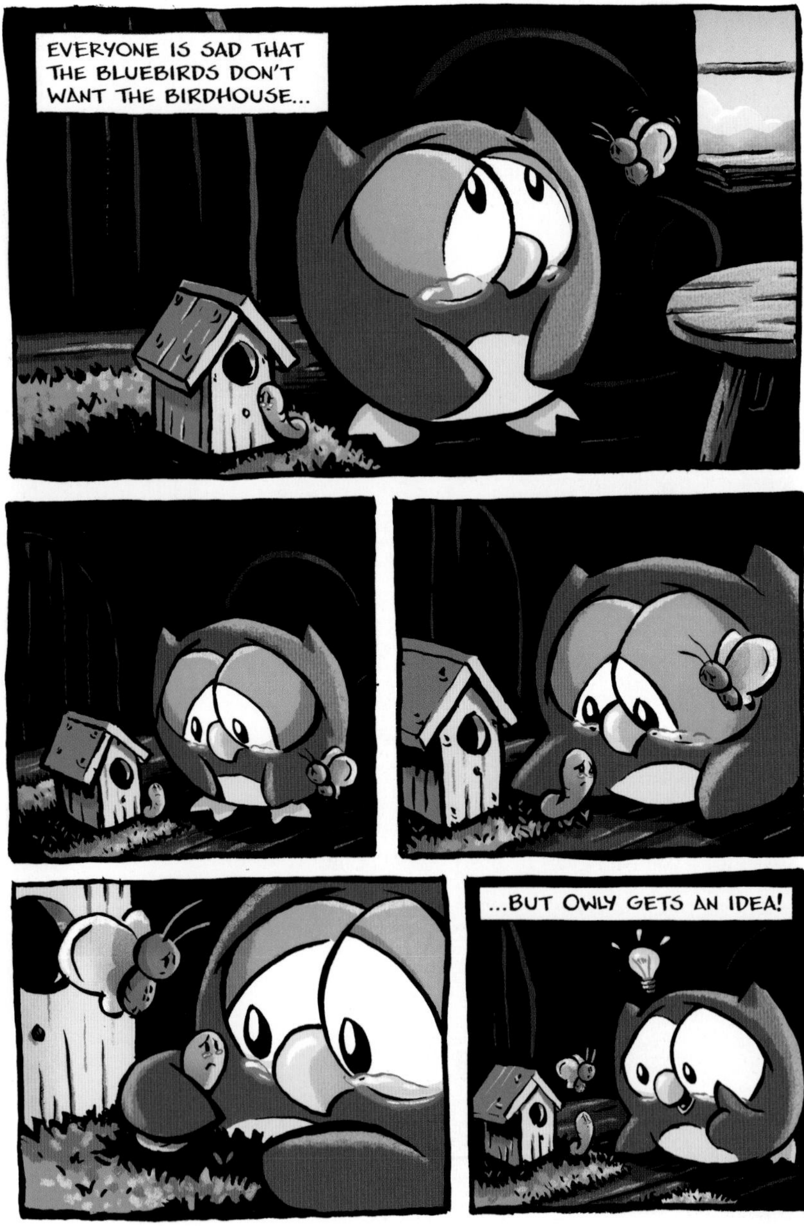
EVERYONE IS SAD THAT THE BLUEBIRDS DON'T WANT THE BIRDHOUSE...
...BUT OWLY GETS AN IDEA!

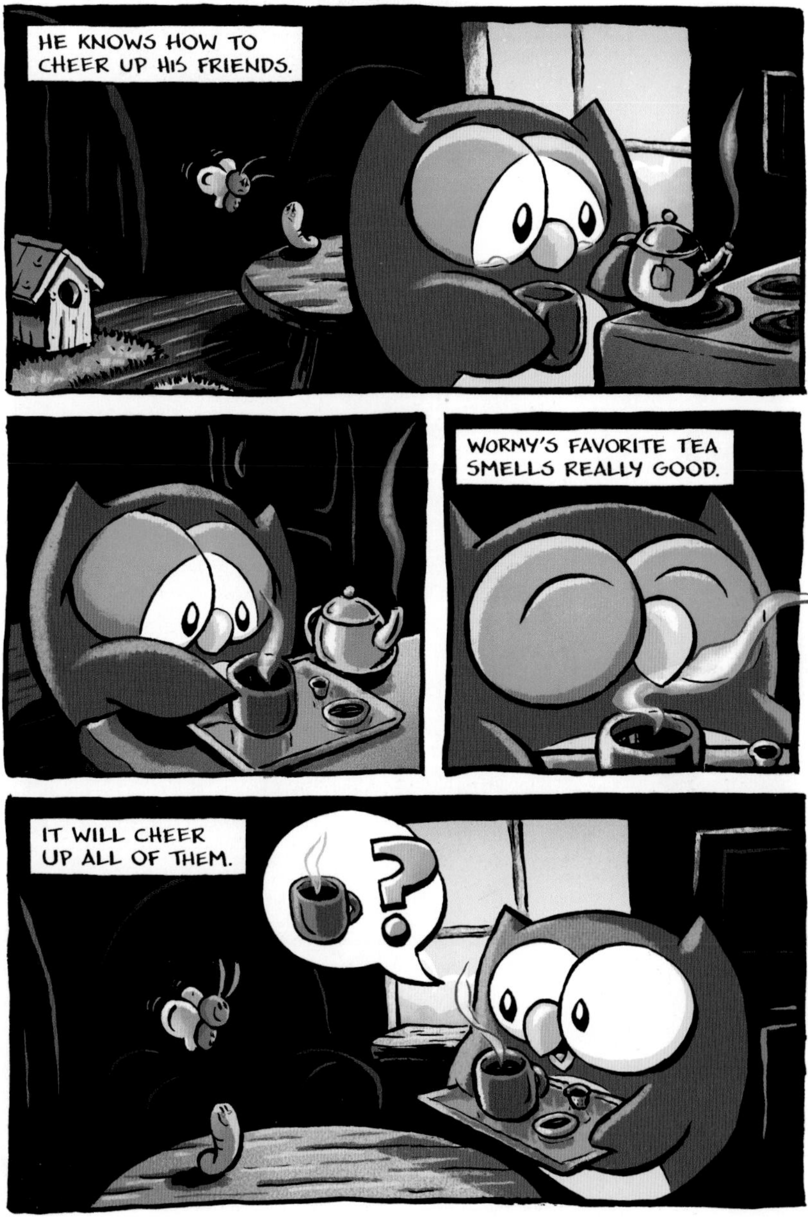
HE KNOWS HOW TO CHEER UP HIS FRIENDS.
WORMY'S FAVORITE TEA SMELLS REALLY GOOD.
IT WILL CHEER UP ALL OF THEM.
?

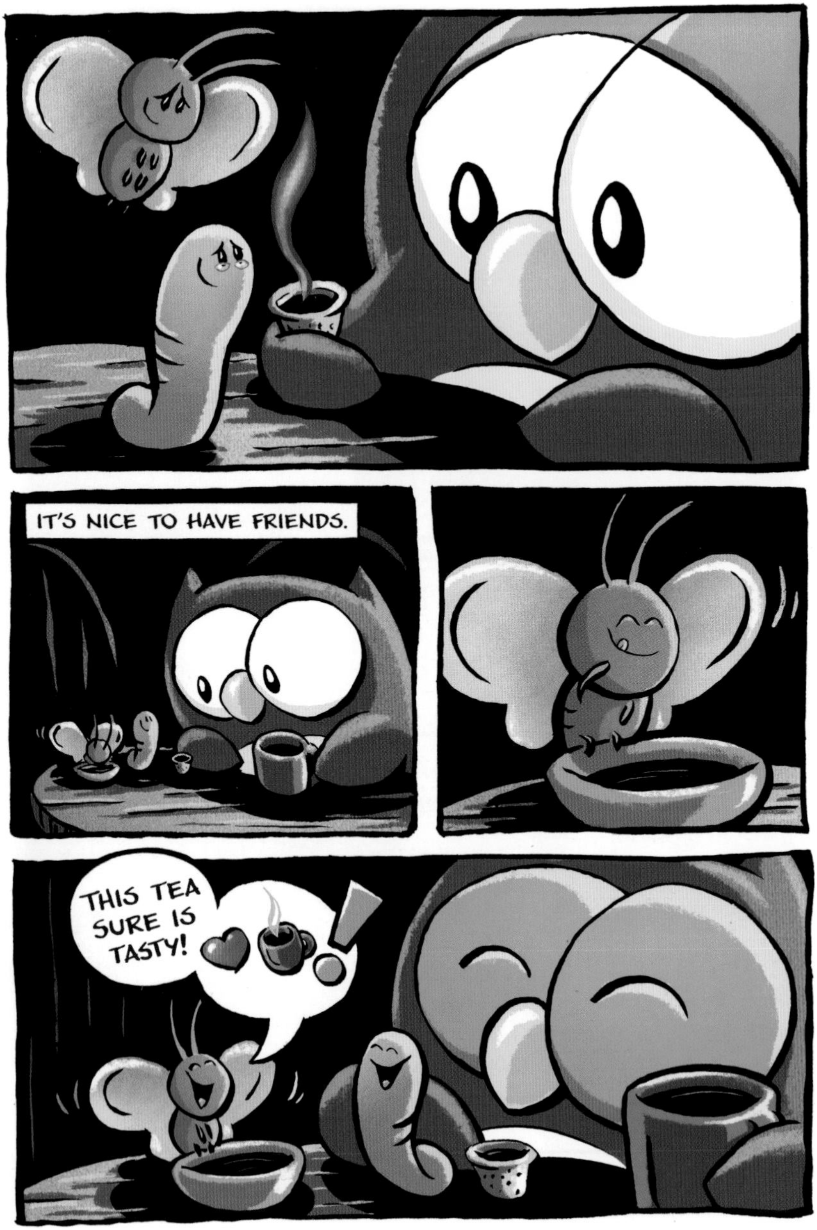
IT'S NICE TO HAVE FRIENDS.
THIS TEA SURE IS TASTY!

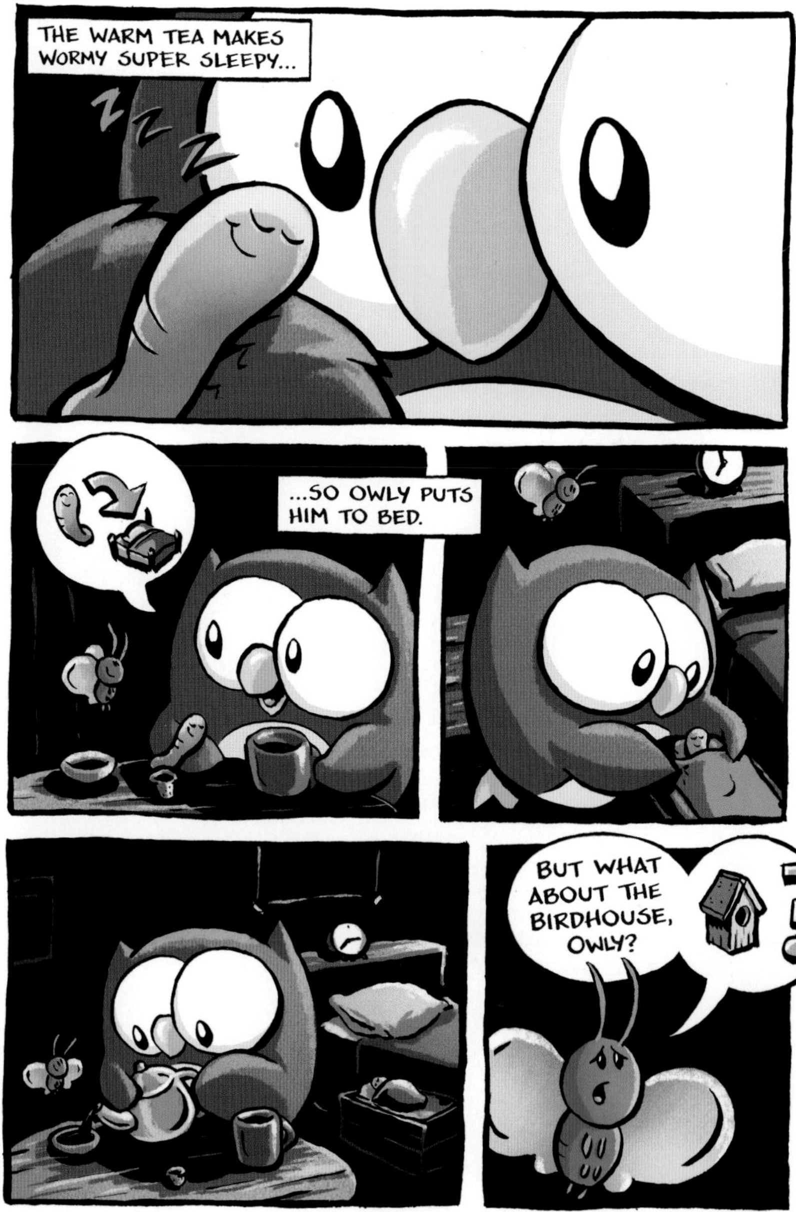
THE WARM TEA MAKES WORMY SUPER SLEEPY...
...SO OWLY PUTS HIM TO BED.
BUT WHAT ABOUT THE BIRDHOUSE, OWLY?

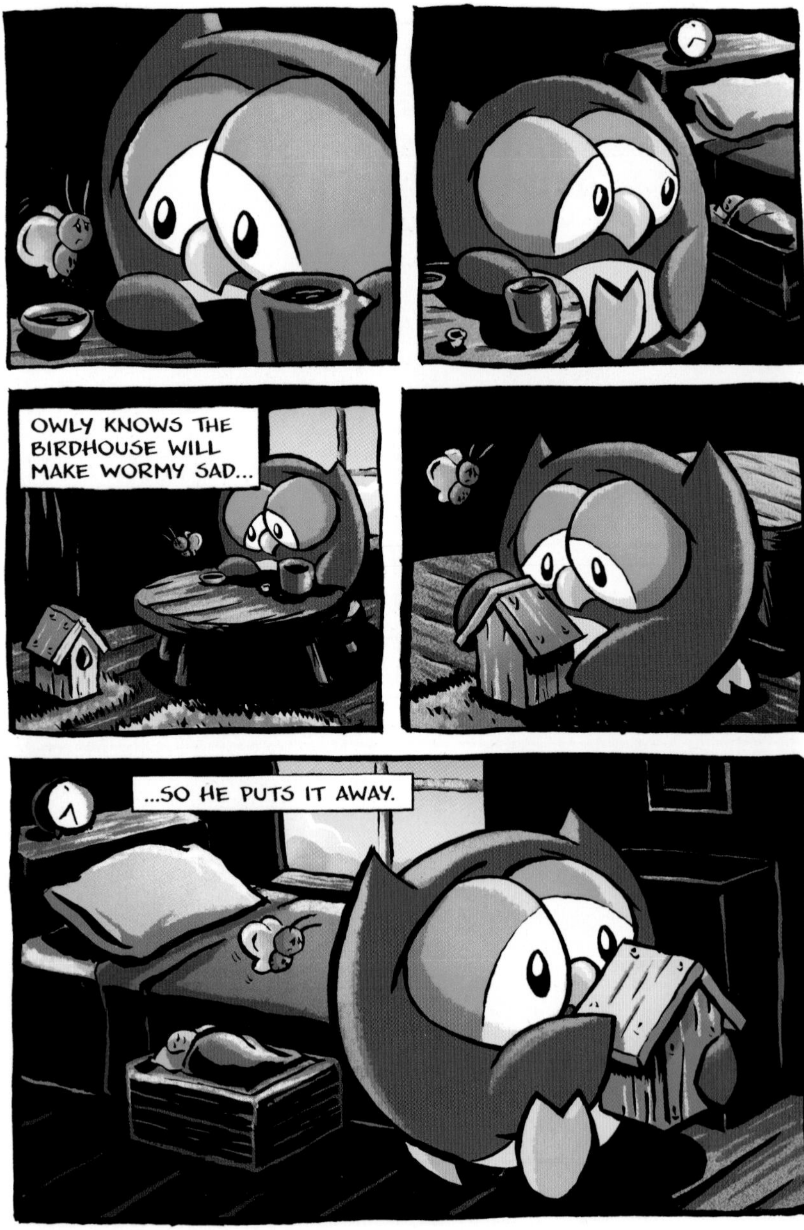
OWLY KNOWS THE BIRDHOUSE WILL MAKE WORMY SAD...
...SO HE PUTS IT AWAY.

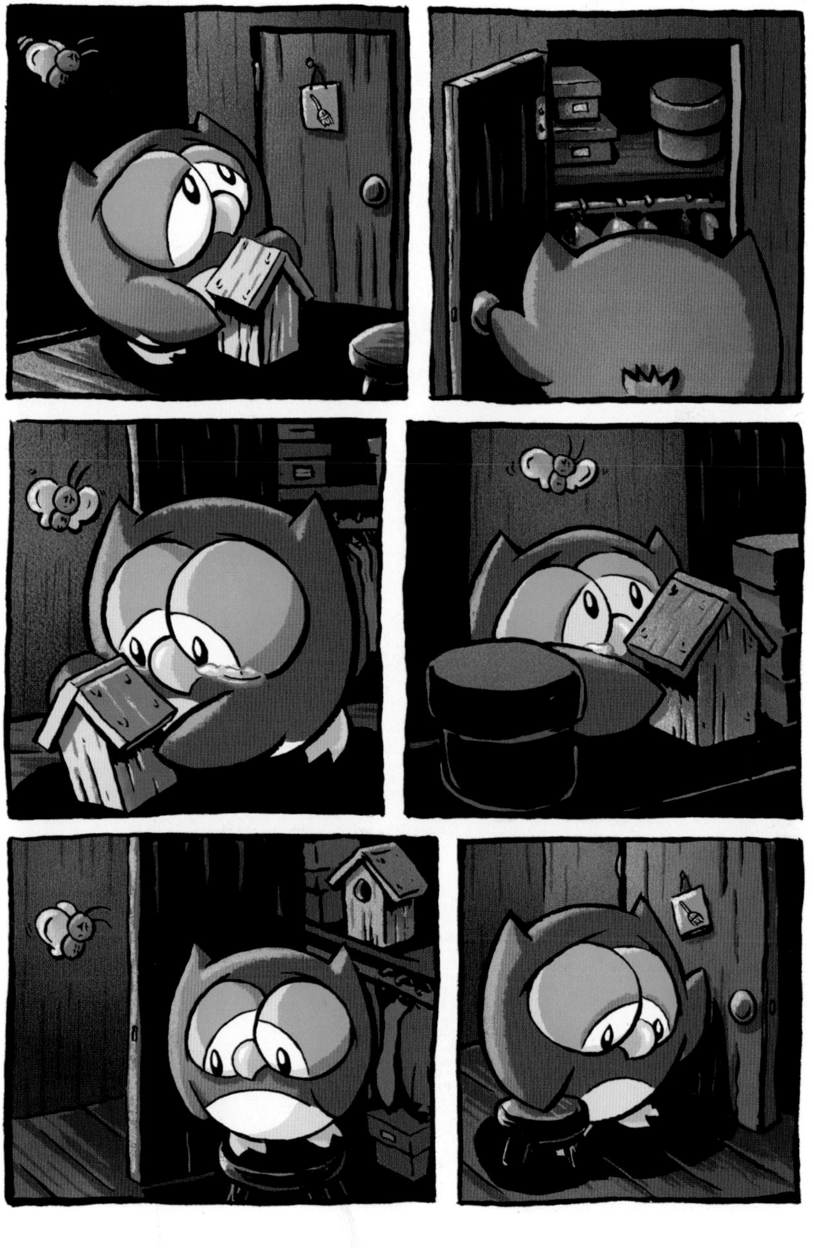

AFTER A WHILE, THE BIRDHOUSE GETS A NEW FRIEND.

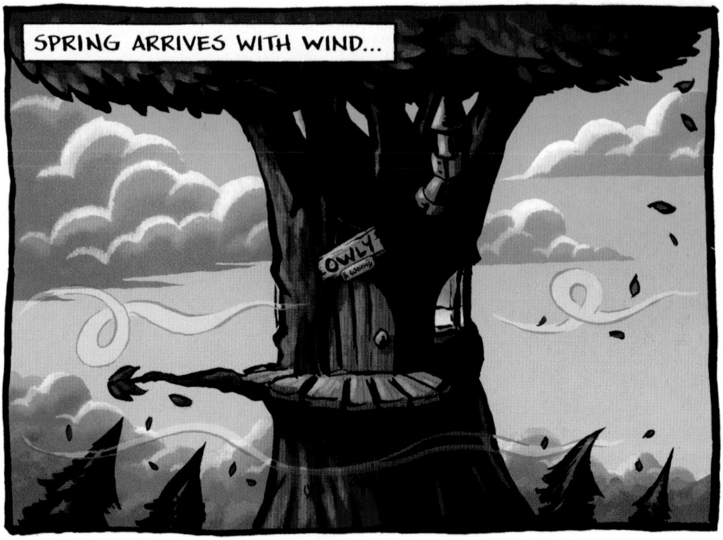
SPRING ARRIVES WITH WIND...
OWLY

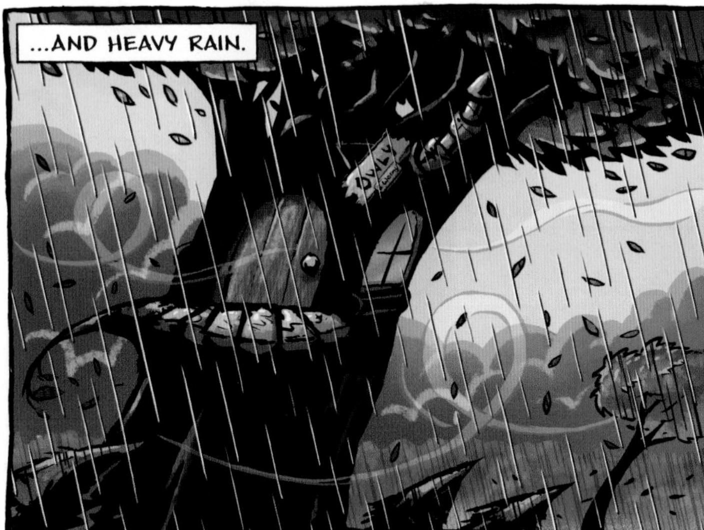
...AND HEAVY RAIN.

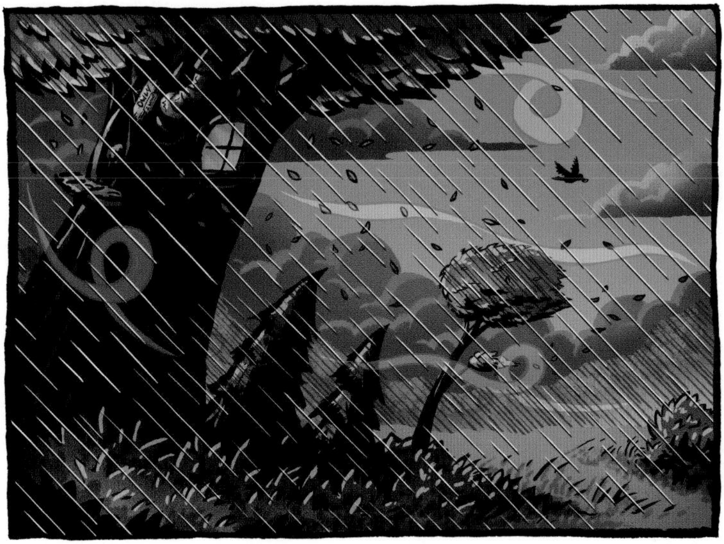
OWLY

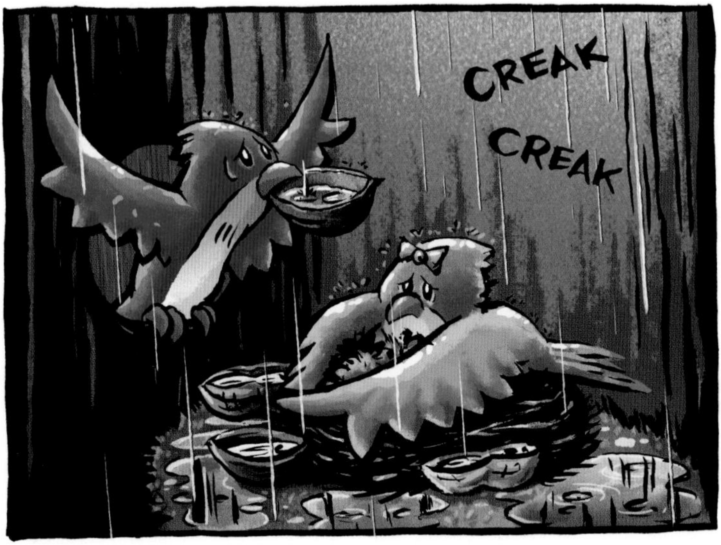
CREAK
CREAK

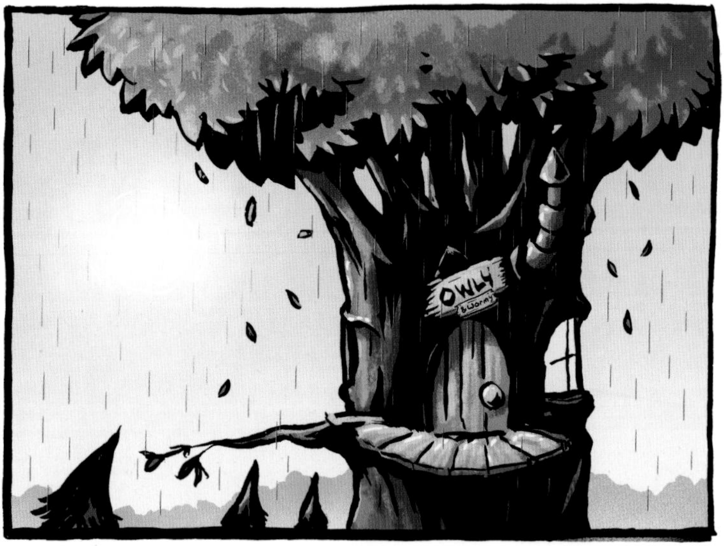
OWLY
& Wormy

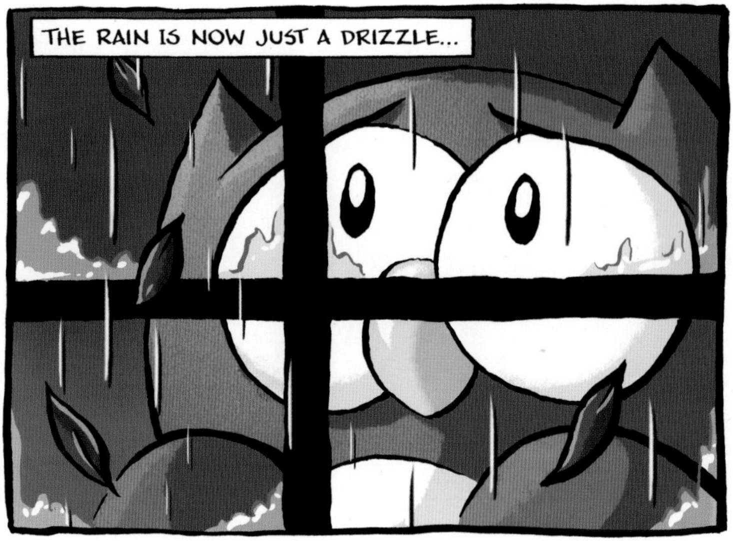
THE RAIN IS NOW JUST A DRIZZLE...

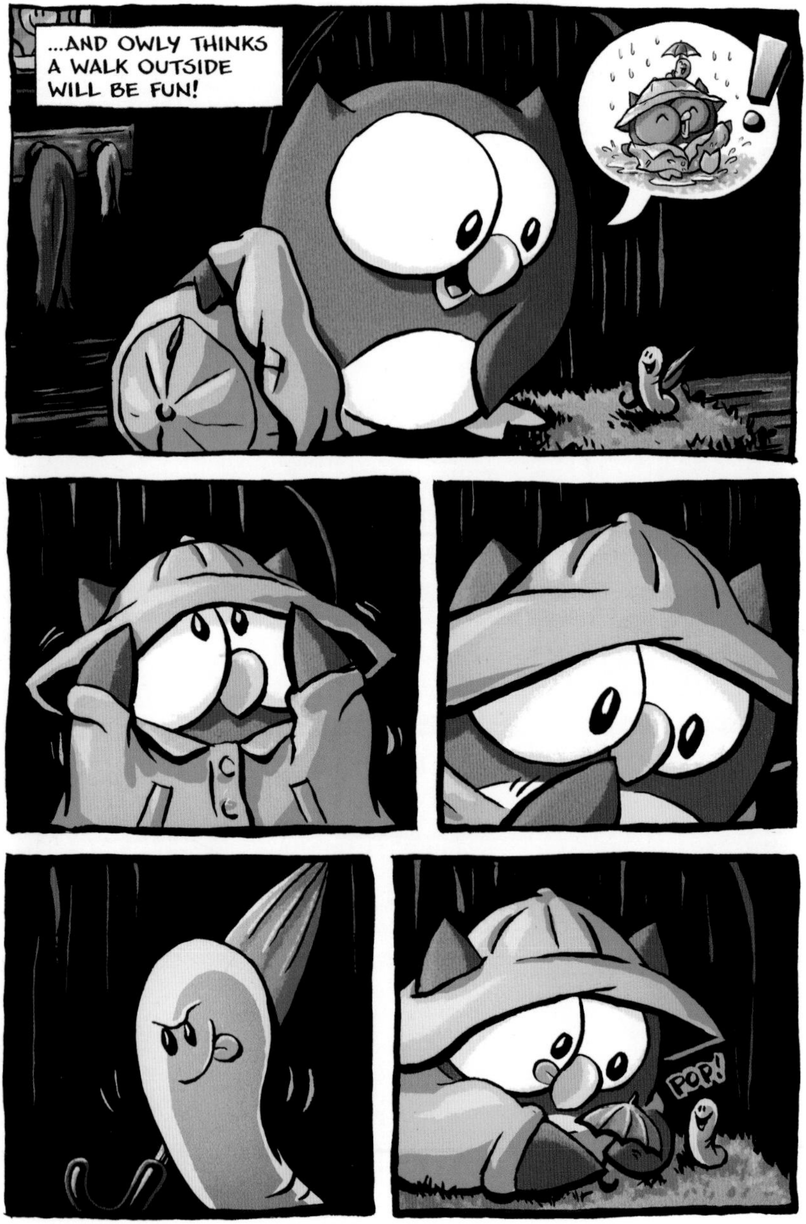
...AND OWLY THINKS A WALK OUTSIDE WILL BE FUN!
!
POP!

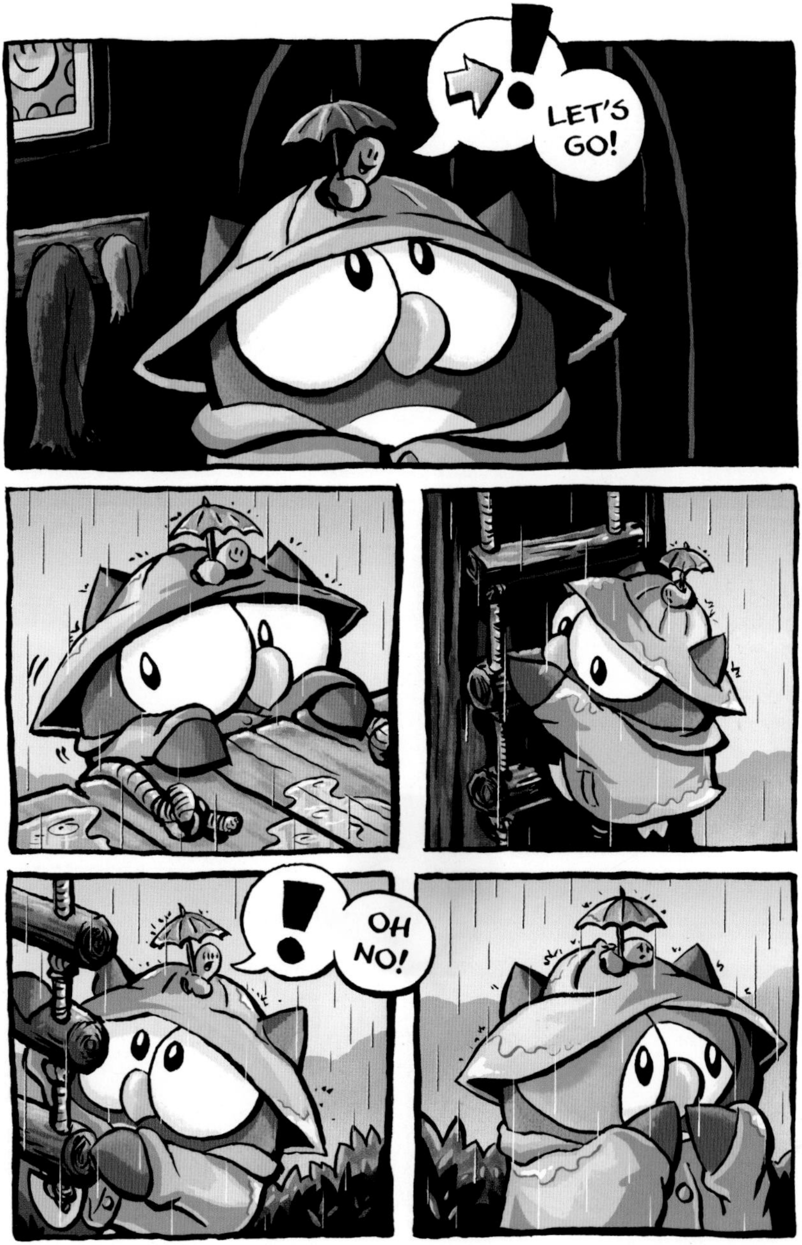
!
LET'S GO!
!
OH NO!

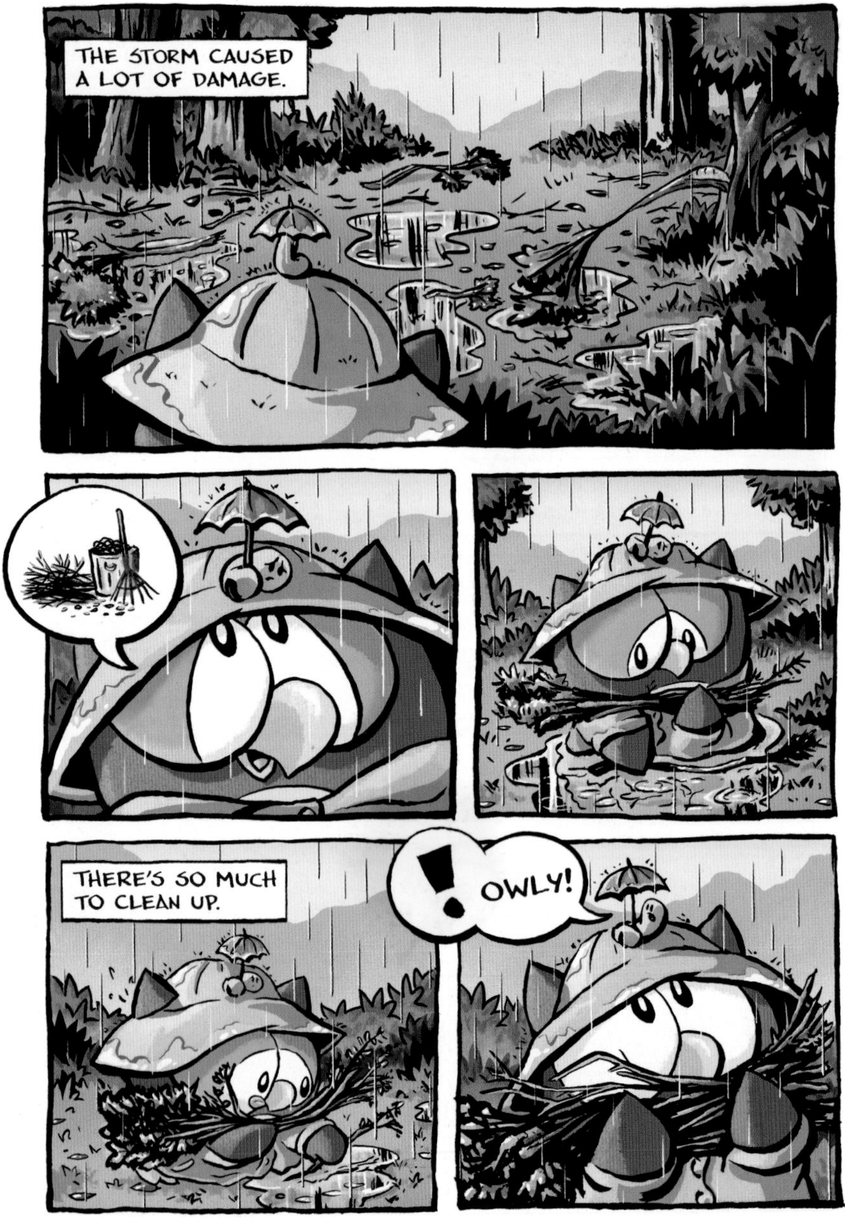
THE STORM CAUSED A LOT OF DAMAGE.
THERE'S SO MUCH TO CLEAN UP.
!
OWLY!

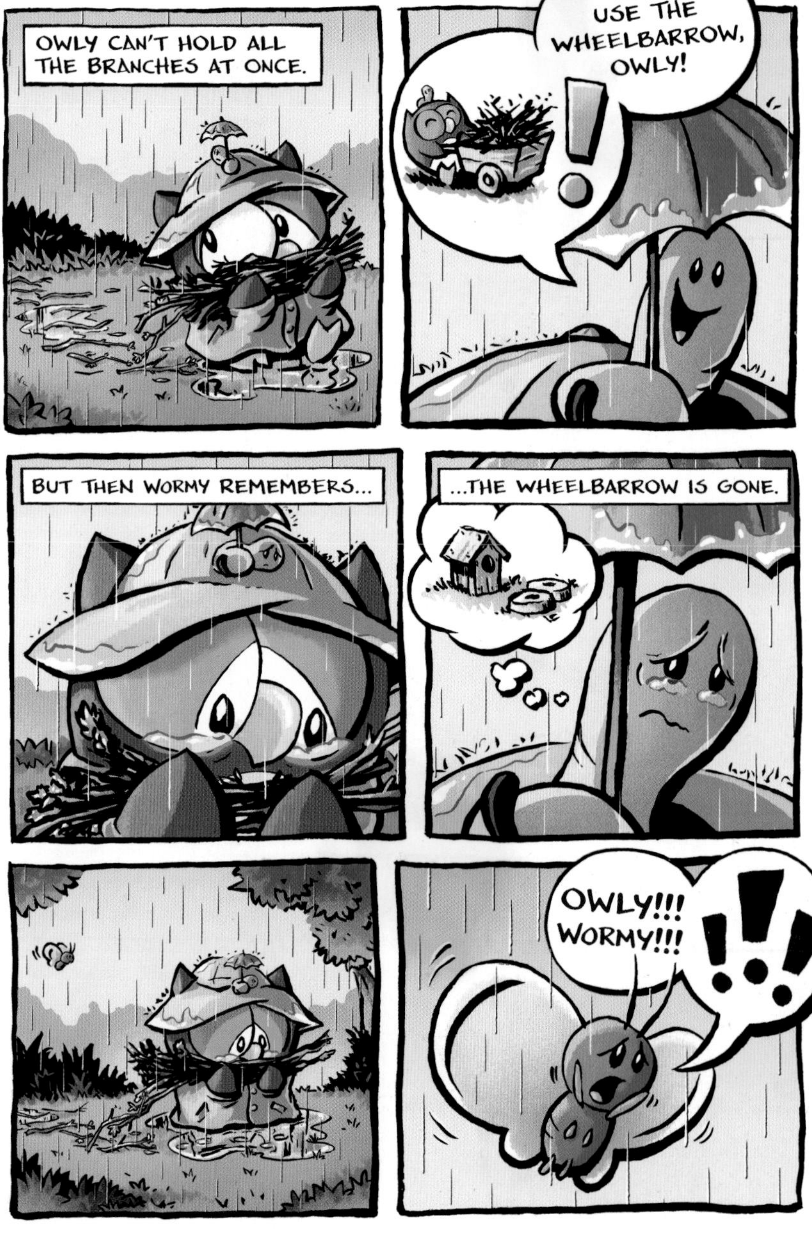
OWLY CAN'T HOLD ALL THE BRANCHES AT ONCE.
LET'S USE THE WHEELBARROW, OWLY!
!
BUT THEN WORMY REMEMBERS...
...THE WHEELBARROW IS GONE.
OWLY!!! WORMY!!!
!!

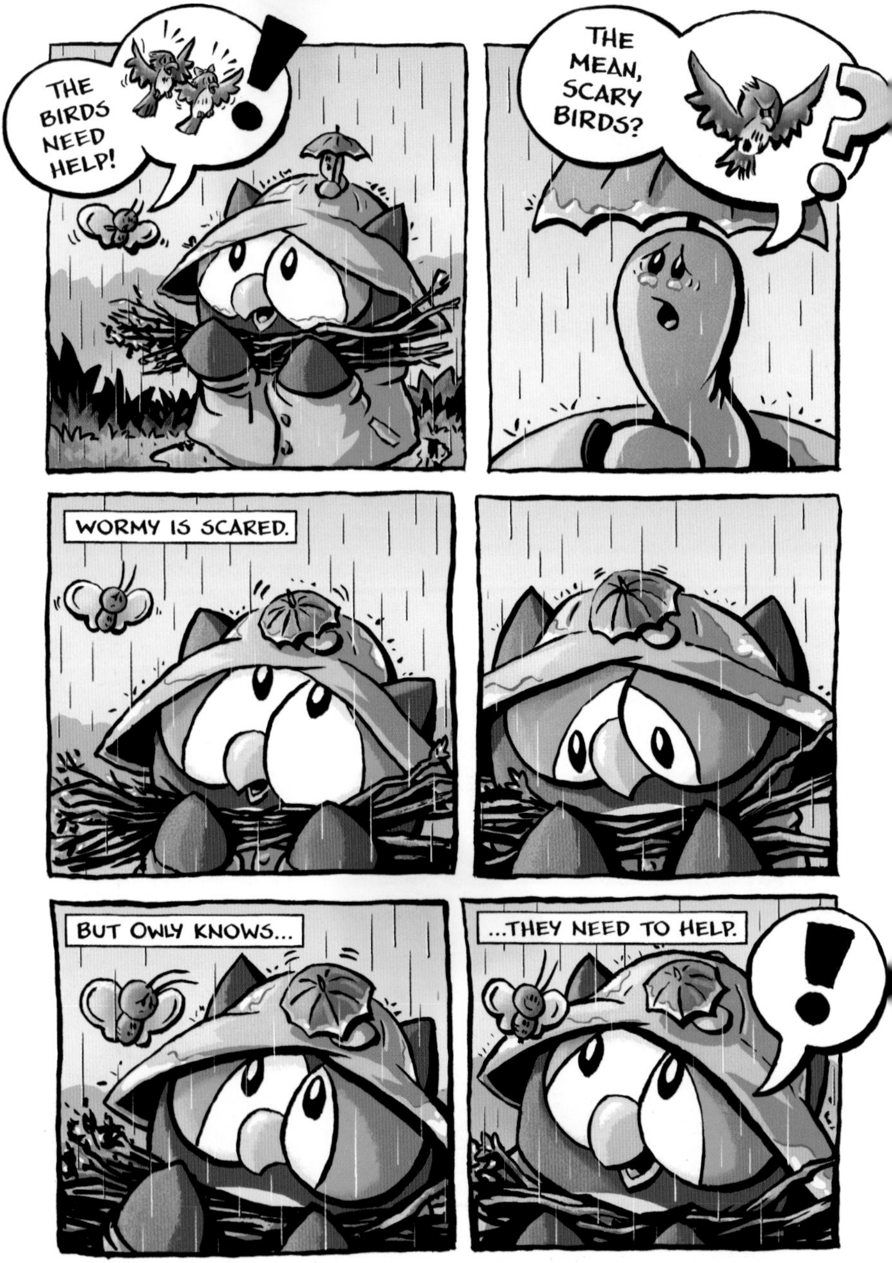
THE BIRDS NEED HELP!
THE MEAN, SCARY BIRDS?
WORMY IS SCARED.
BUT OWLY KNOWS...
...THEY NEED TO HELP.

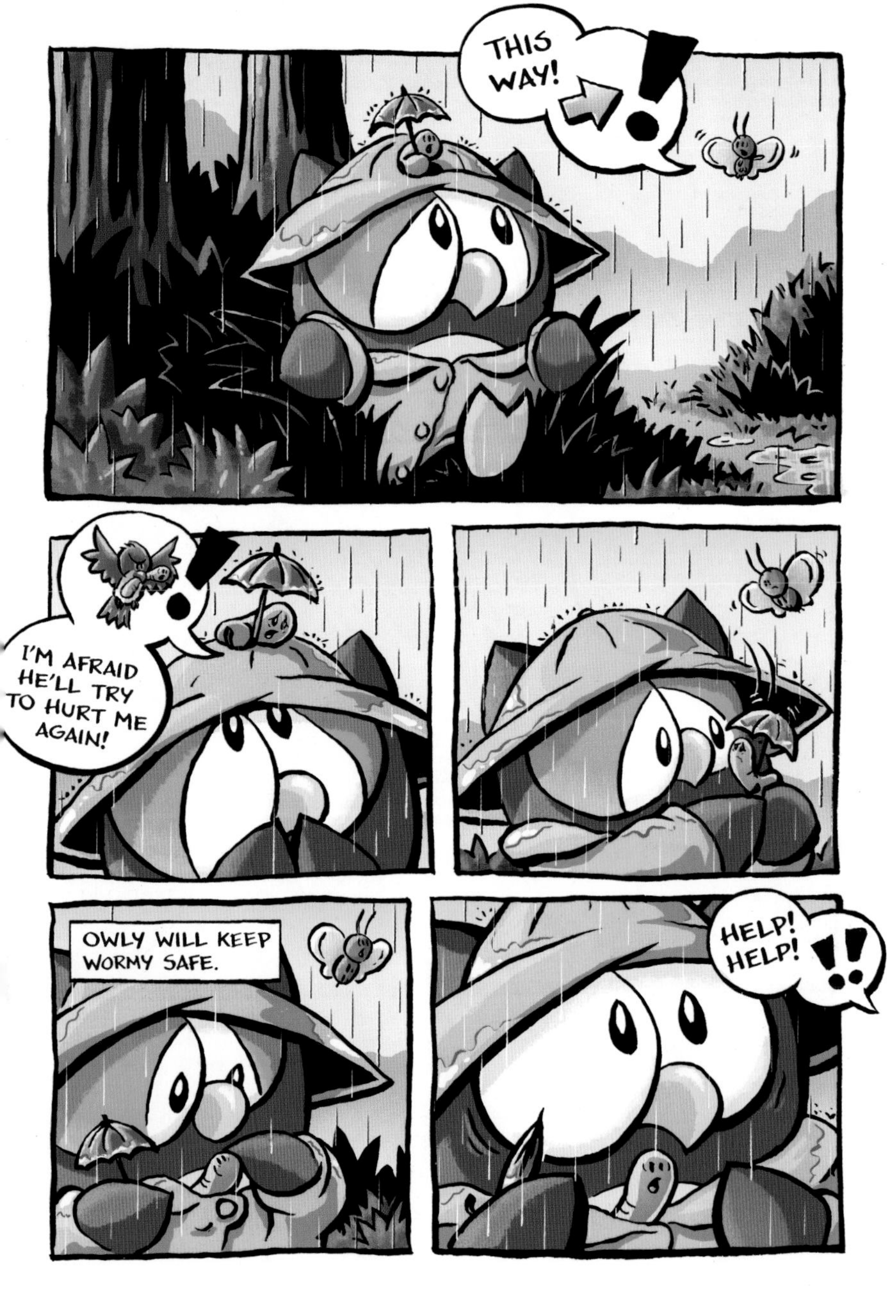
THIS WAY!
I'M AFRAID HE'LL TRY TO HURT ME AGAIN!
OWLY WILL KEEP WORMY SAFE.
HELP! HELP!

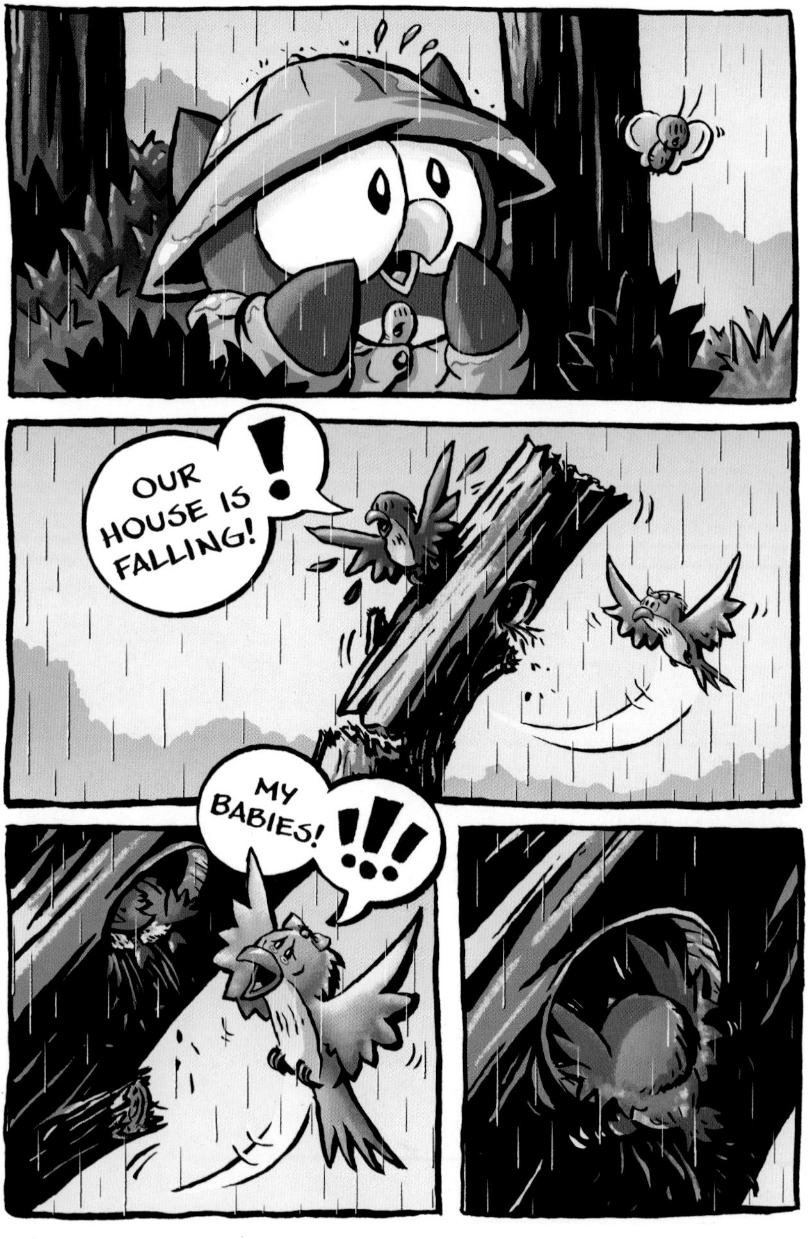
OUR HOUSE IS FALLING!
MY BABIES!

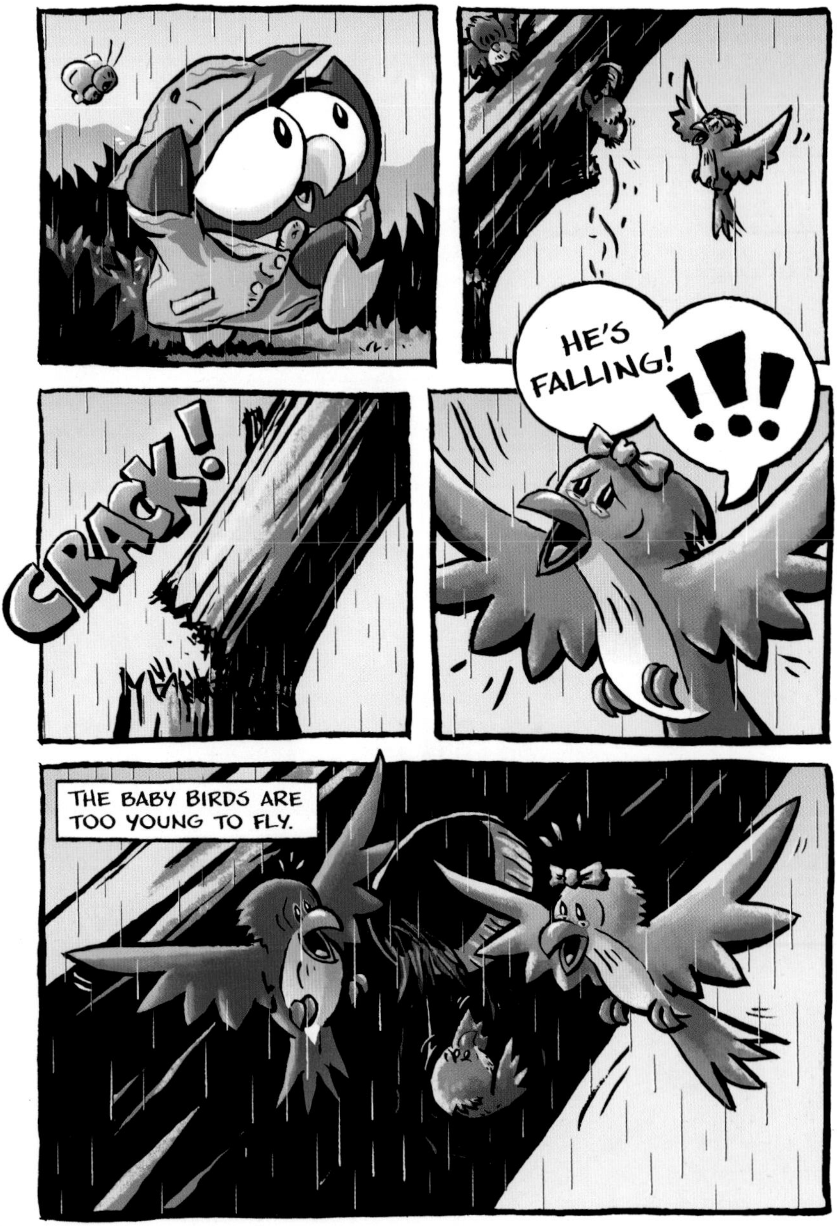

CRACK!
HE'S FALLING!
!!!
THE BABY BIRDS ARE TOO YOUNG TO FLY.

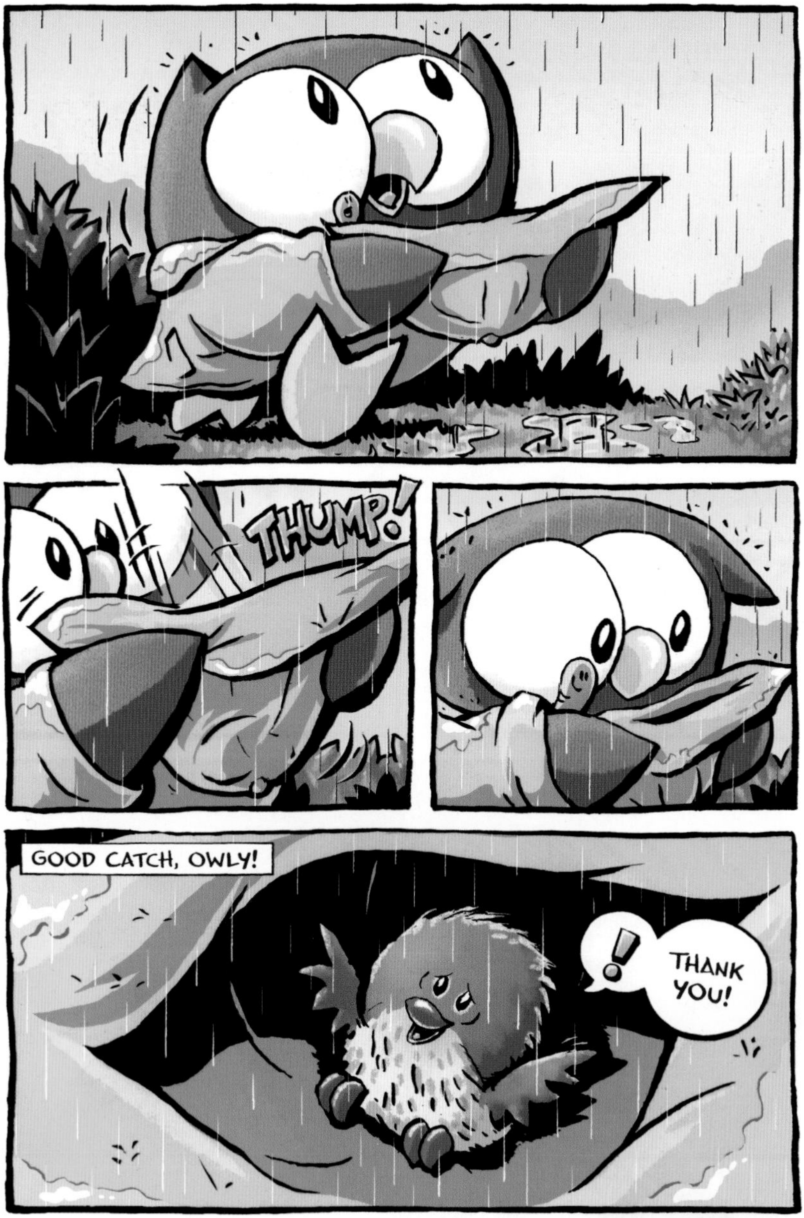
THUMP!
GOOD CATCH, OWLY!
!
THANK YOU!

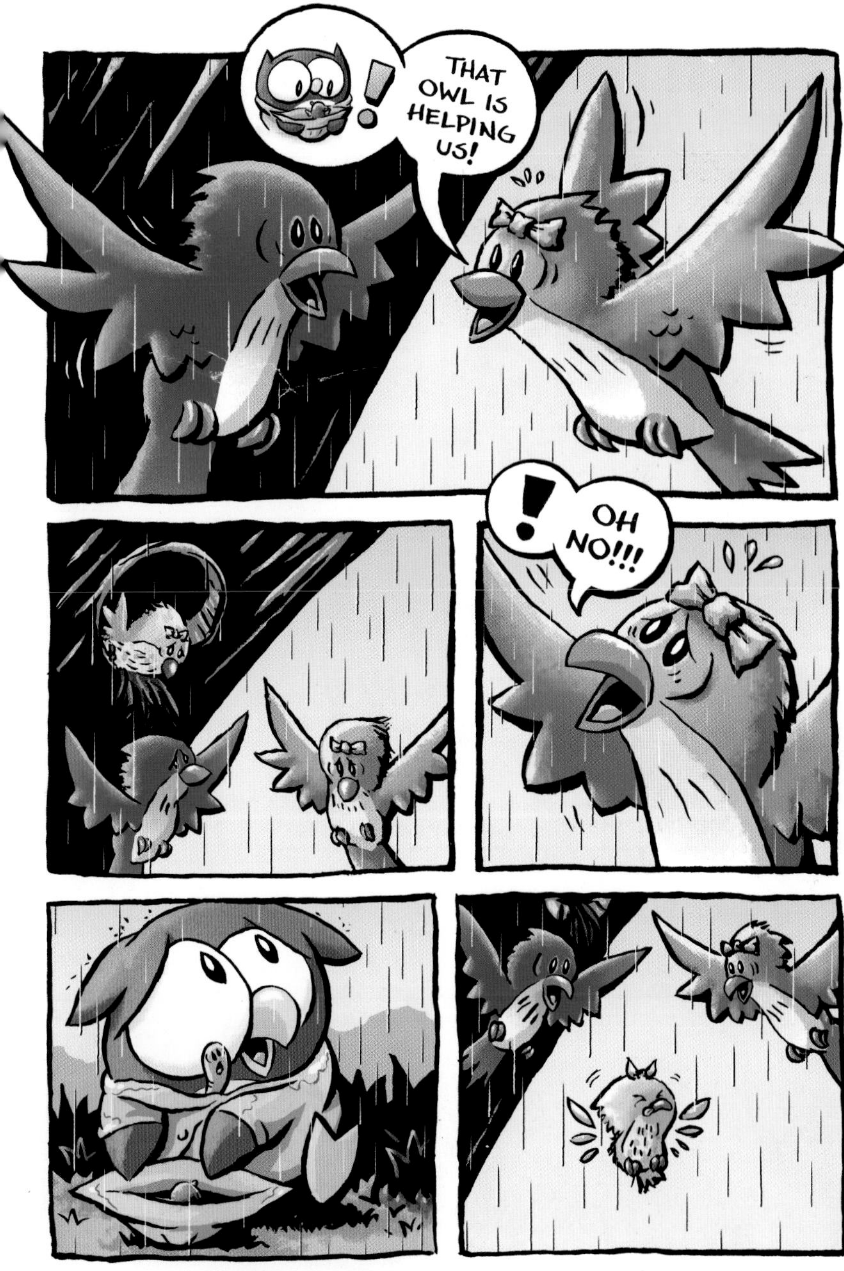
!
THAT OWL IS HELPING US!
!
OH NO!!!

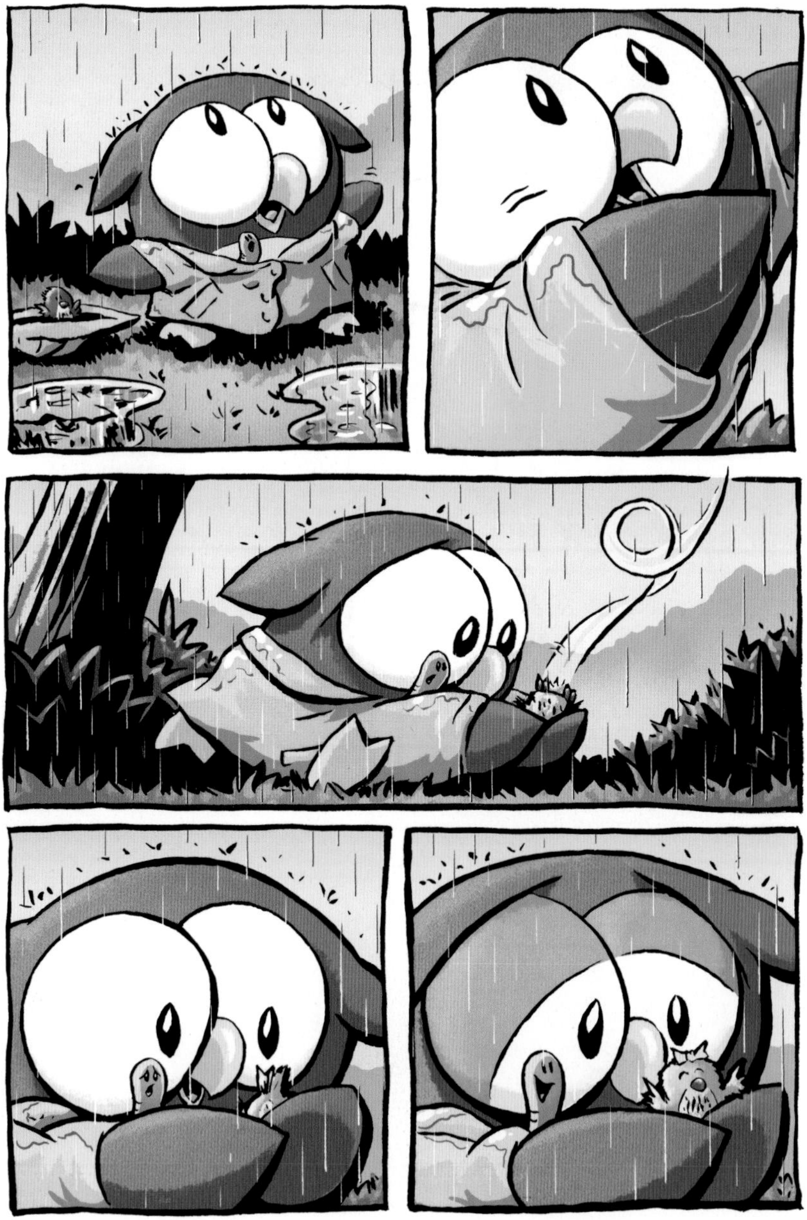

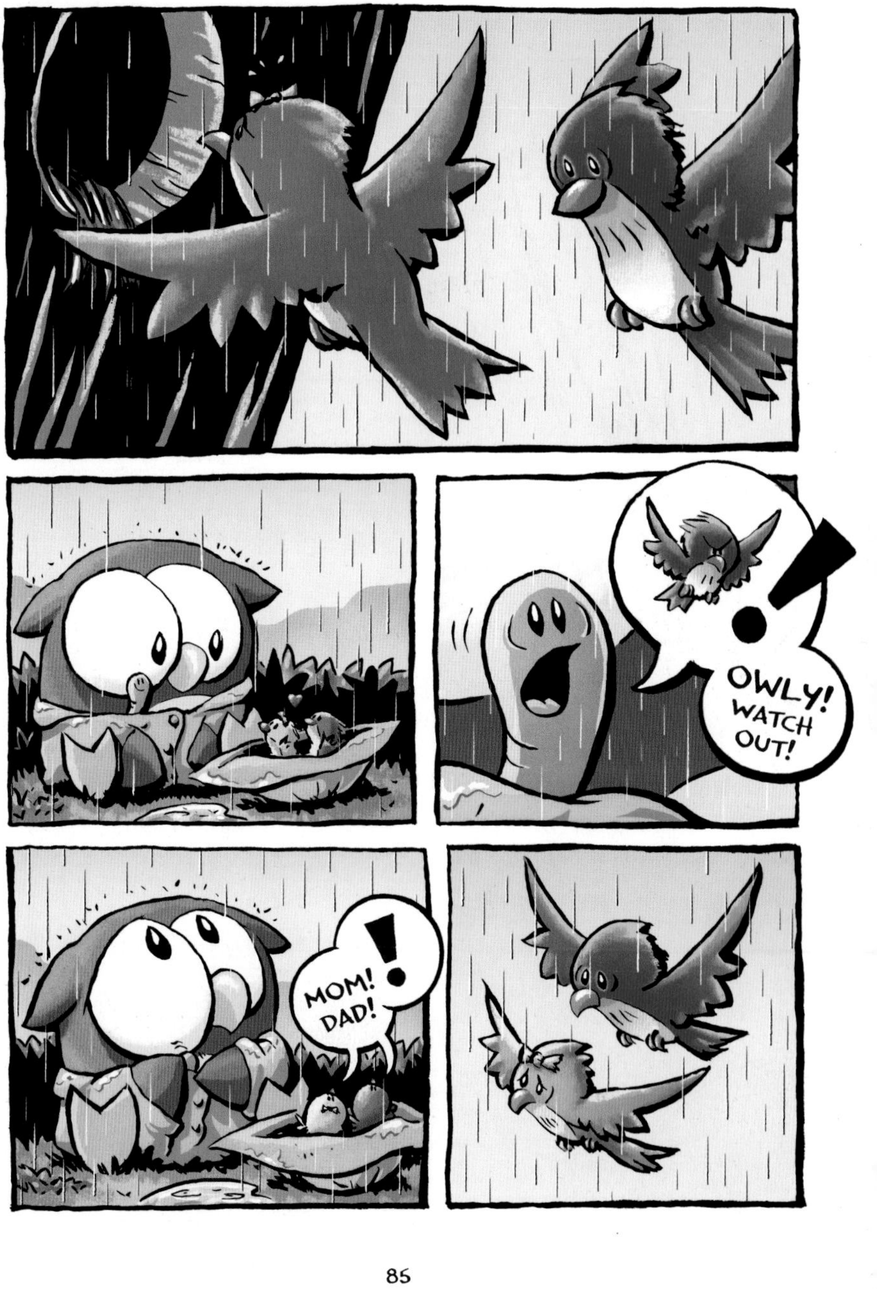
!
OWLY! WATCH OUT!
MOM! DAD!
!

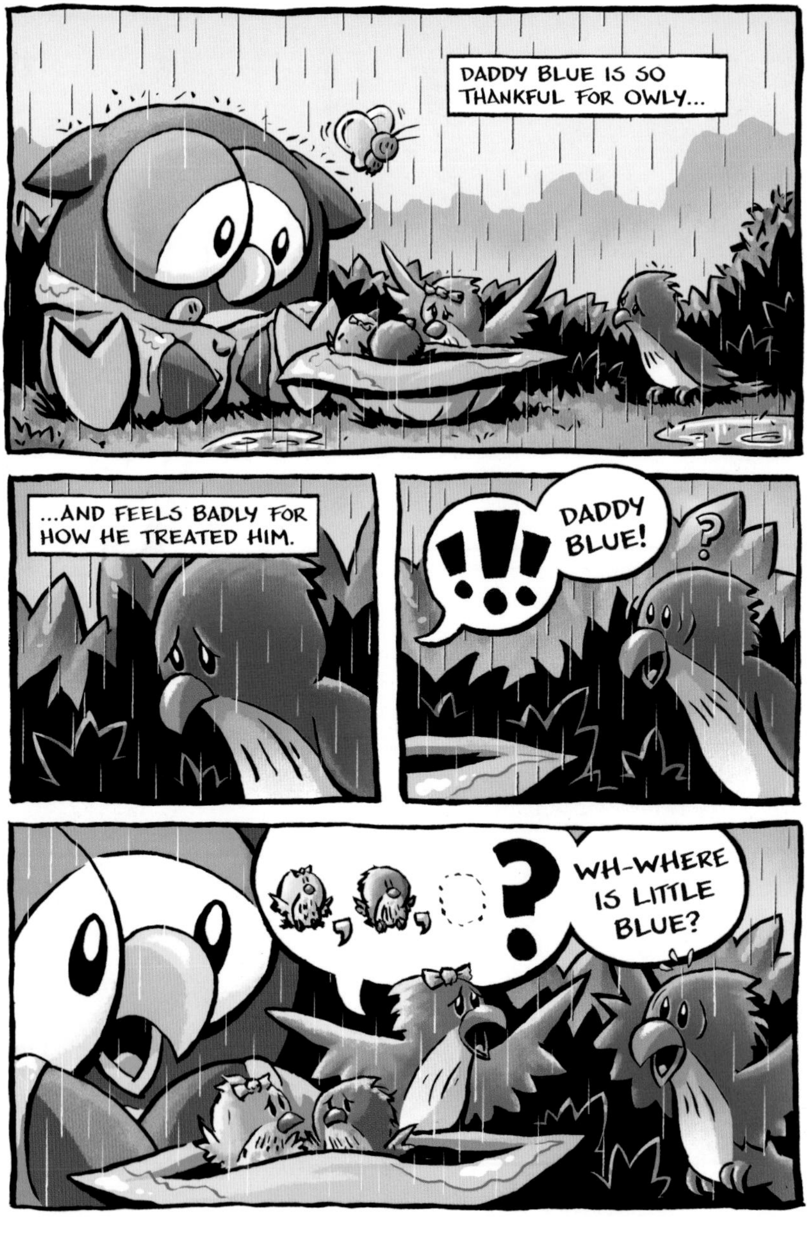
DADDY BLUE IS SO THANKFUL FOR OWLY...
...AND FEELS BADLY FOR HOW HE TREATED HIM.
!!!
DADDY BLUE!
?
?
WH-WHERE IS LITTLE BLUE?

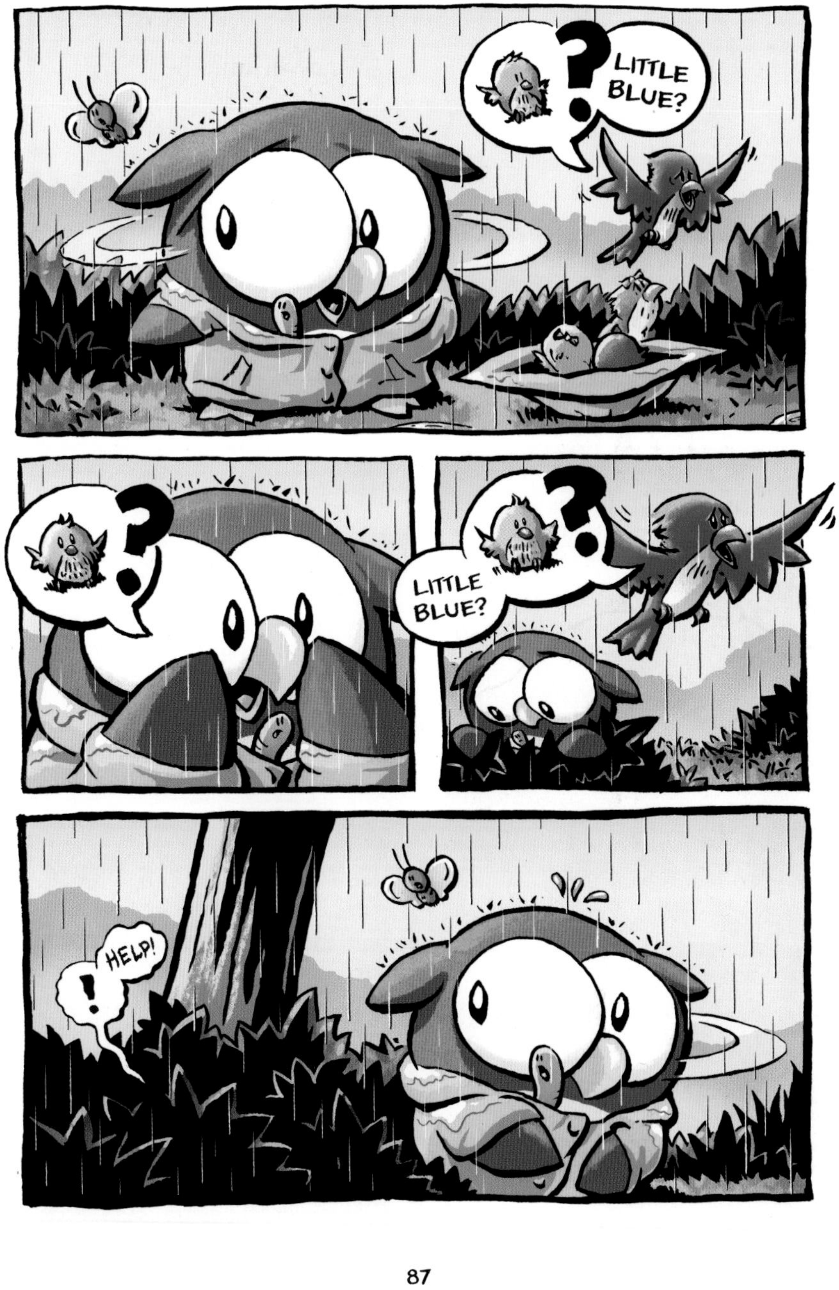
LITTLE BLUE?
LITTLE BLUE?
HELP!

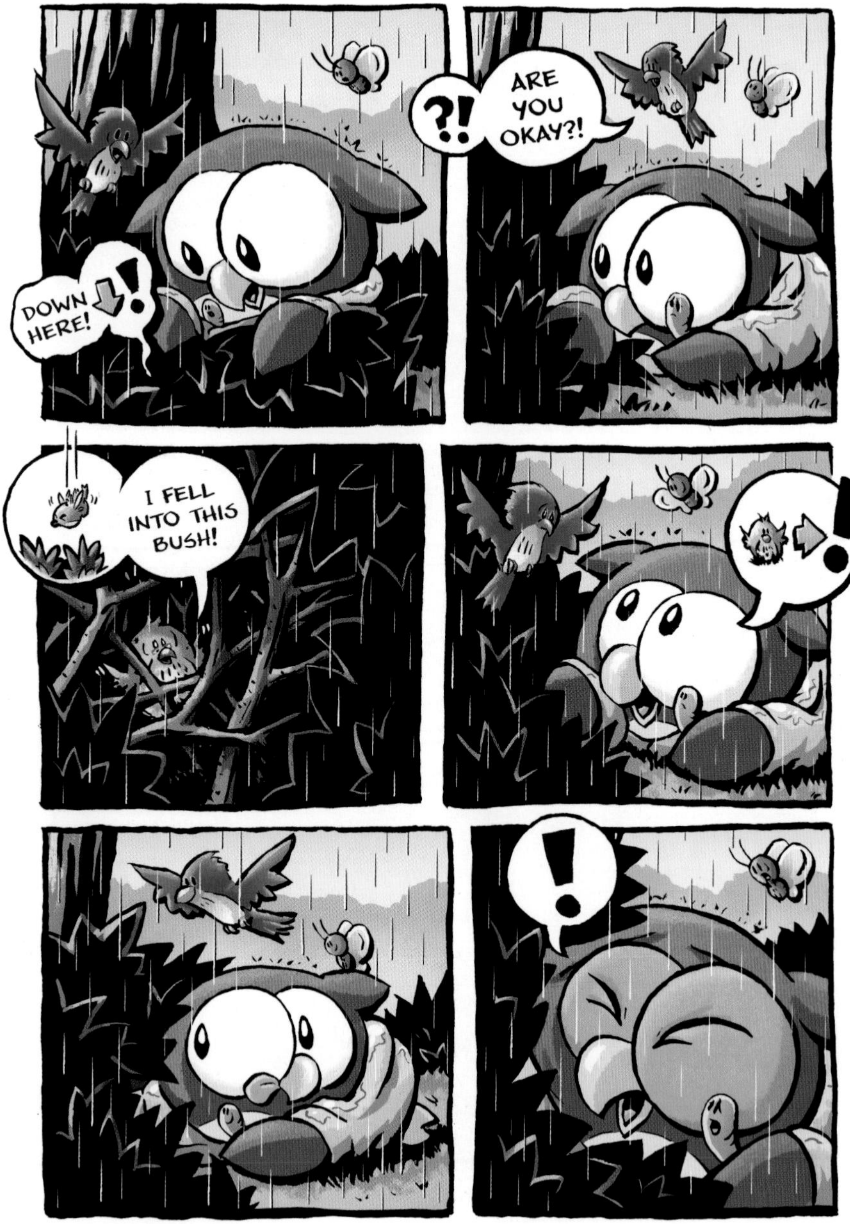
DOWN HERE!
?!
ARE YOU OKAY?!
I FELL INTO THIS BUSH!

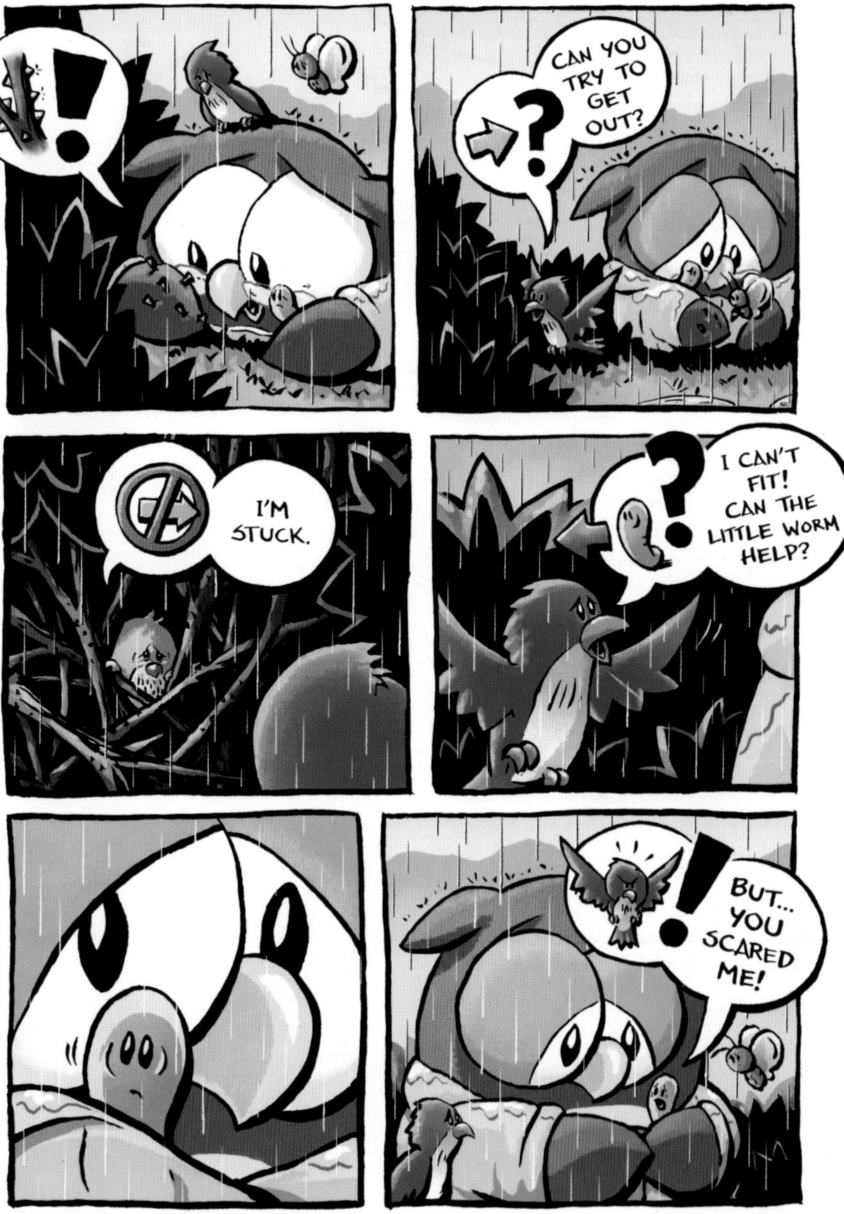
!
CAN YOU TRY TO GET OUT?
I'M STUCK.
I CAN'T FIT! CAN THE LITTLE WORM HELP?
BUT... YOU SCARED ME!

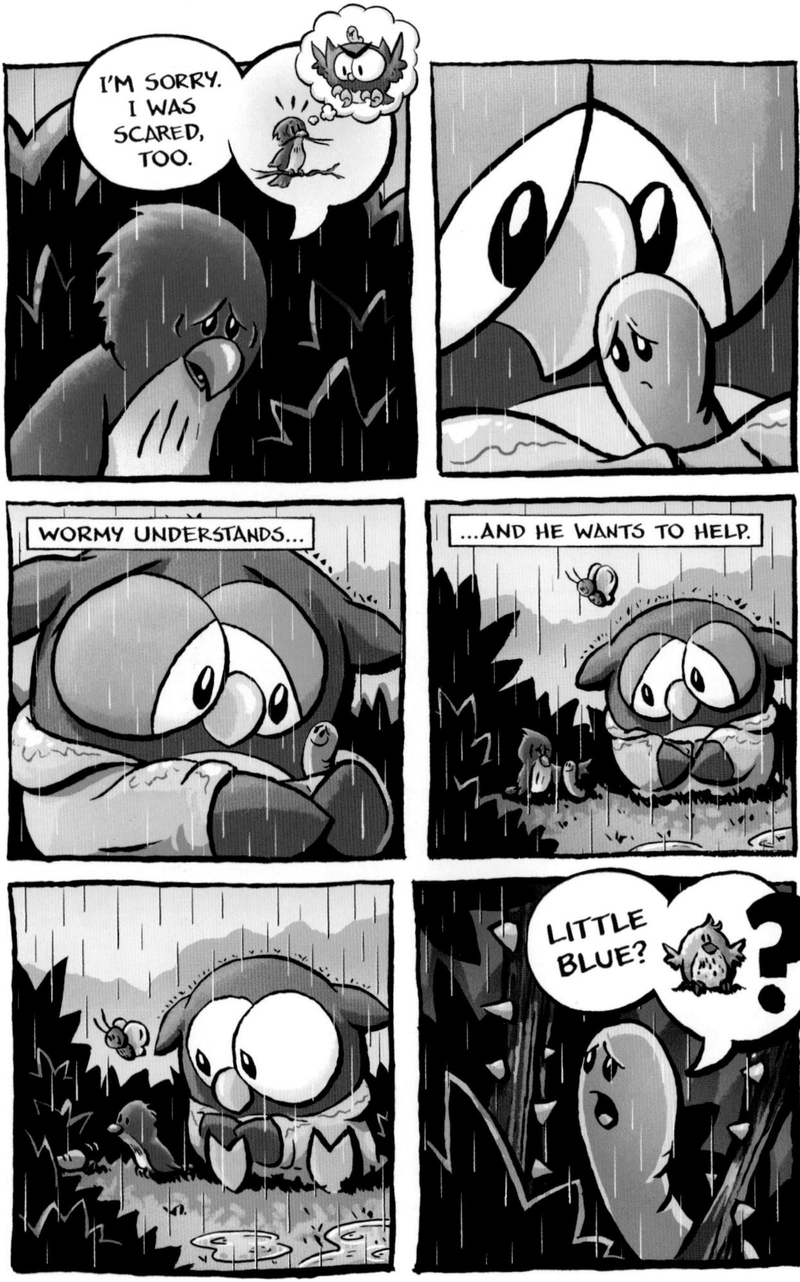
I'M SORRY. I WAS SCARED, TOO.
WORMY UNDERSTANDS...
...AND HE WANTS TO HELP.
LITTLE BLUE?

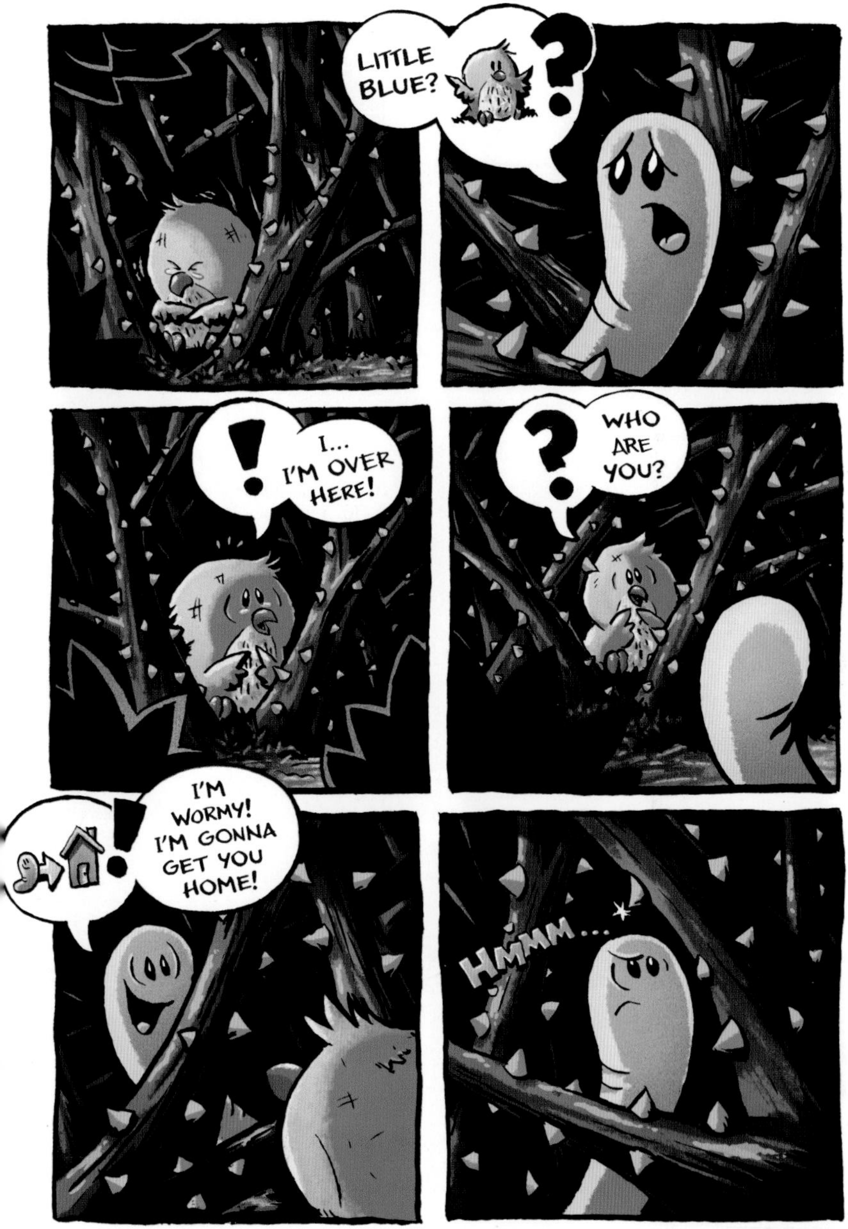
LITTLE BLUE?
I... I'M OVER HERE!
WHO ARE YOU?
I'M WORMY! I'M GONNA GET YOU HOME!
HMMM...

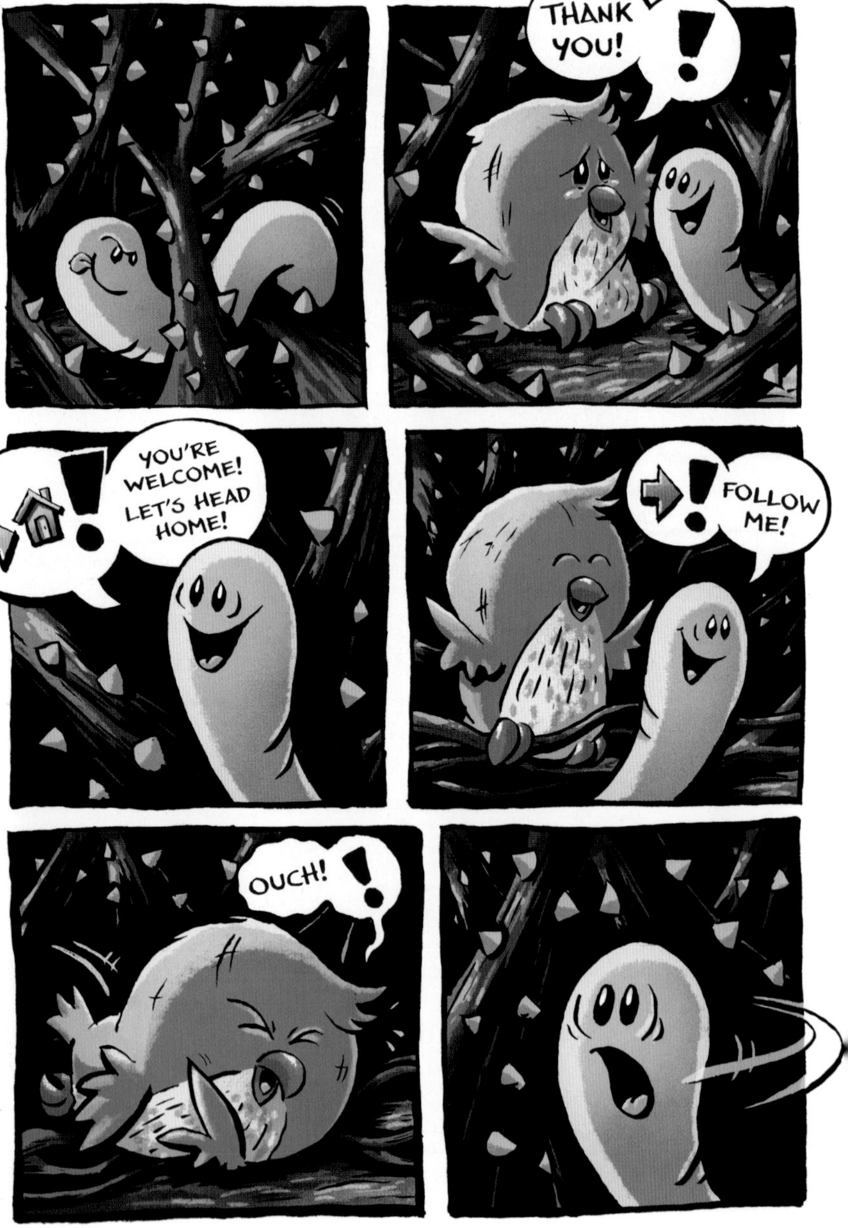
THANK YOU!
!
!
YOU'RE WELCOME! LET'S HEAD HOME!
!
FOLLOW ME!
OUCH!
!

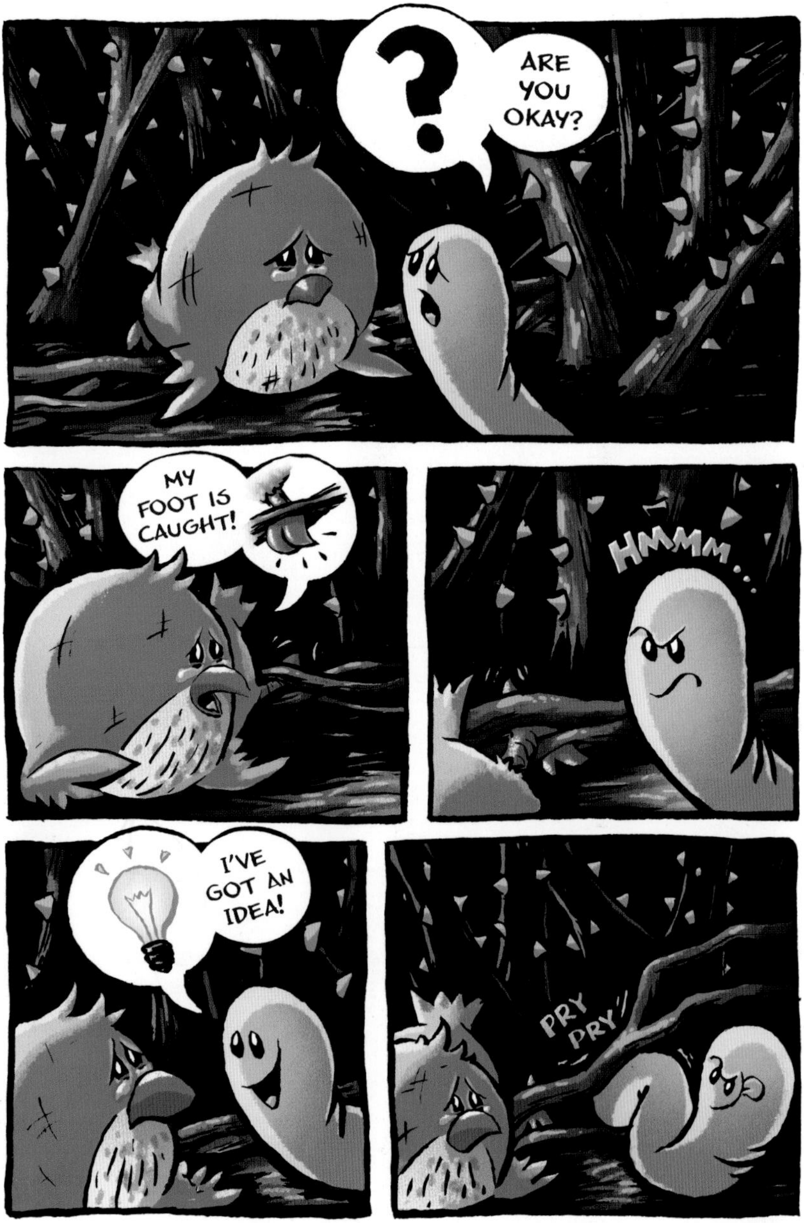
?
ARE YOU OKAY?
MY FOOT IS CAUGHT!
HMMM...
I'VE GOT AN IDEA!
PRY PRY

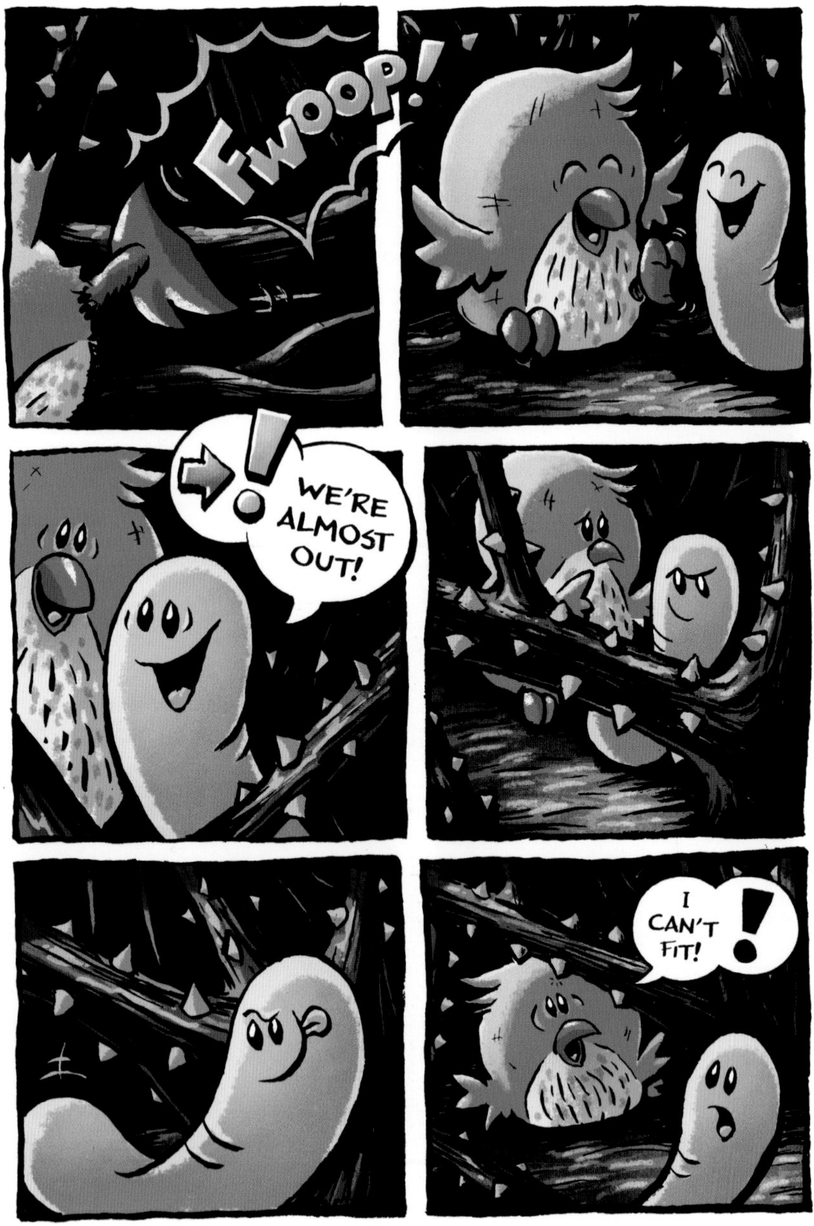
FWOOP!
WE'RE ALMOST OUT!
I CAN'T FIT!

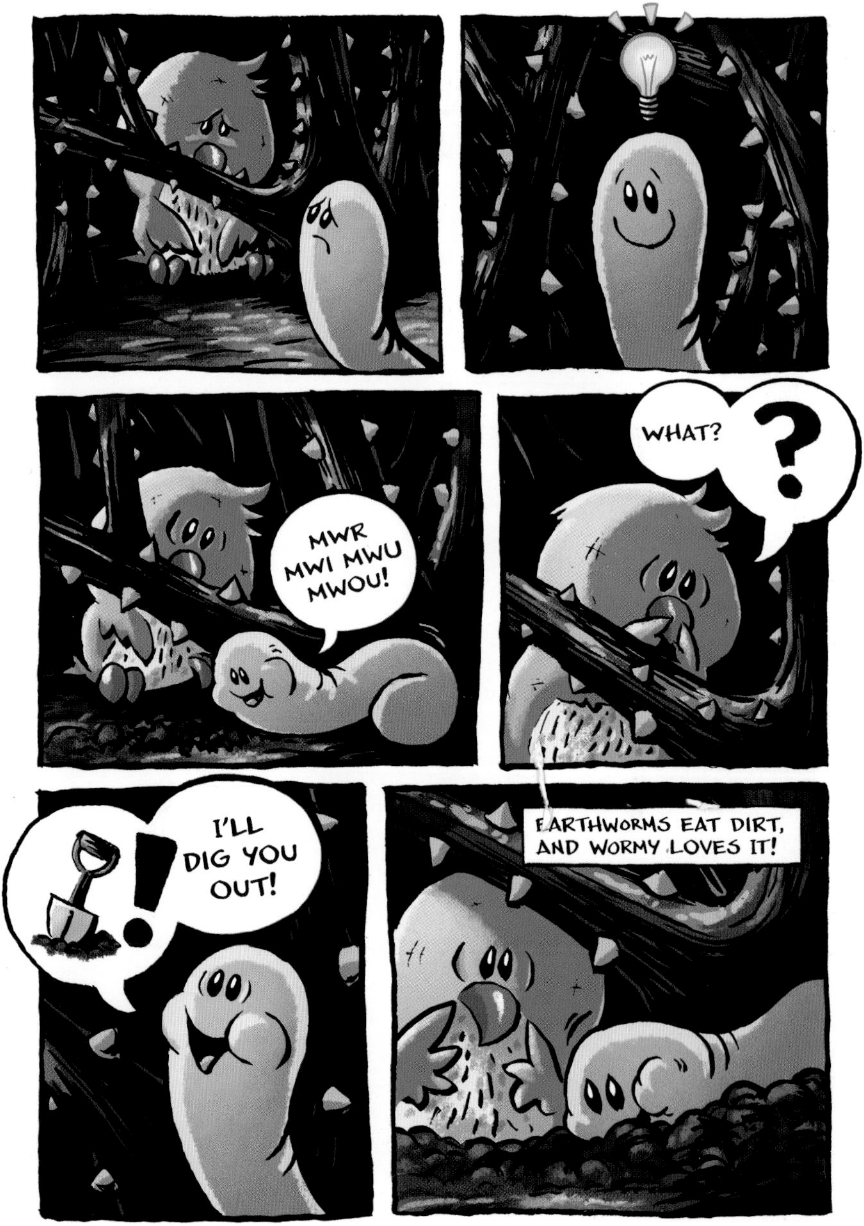
MWR MWI MWU MWOU!
WHAT?
?
I'LL DIG YOU OUT!
!
EARTHWORMS EAT DIRT, AND WORMY LOVES IT!

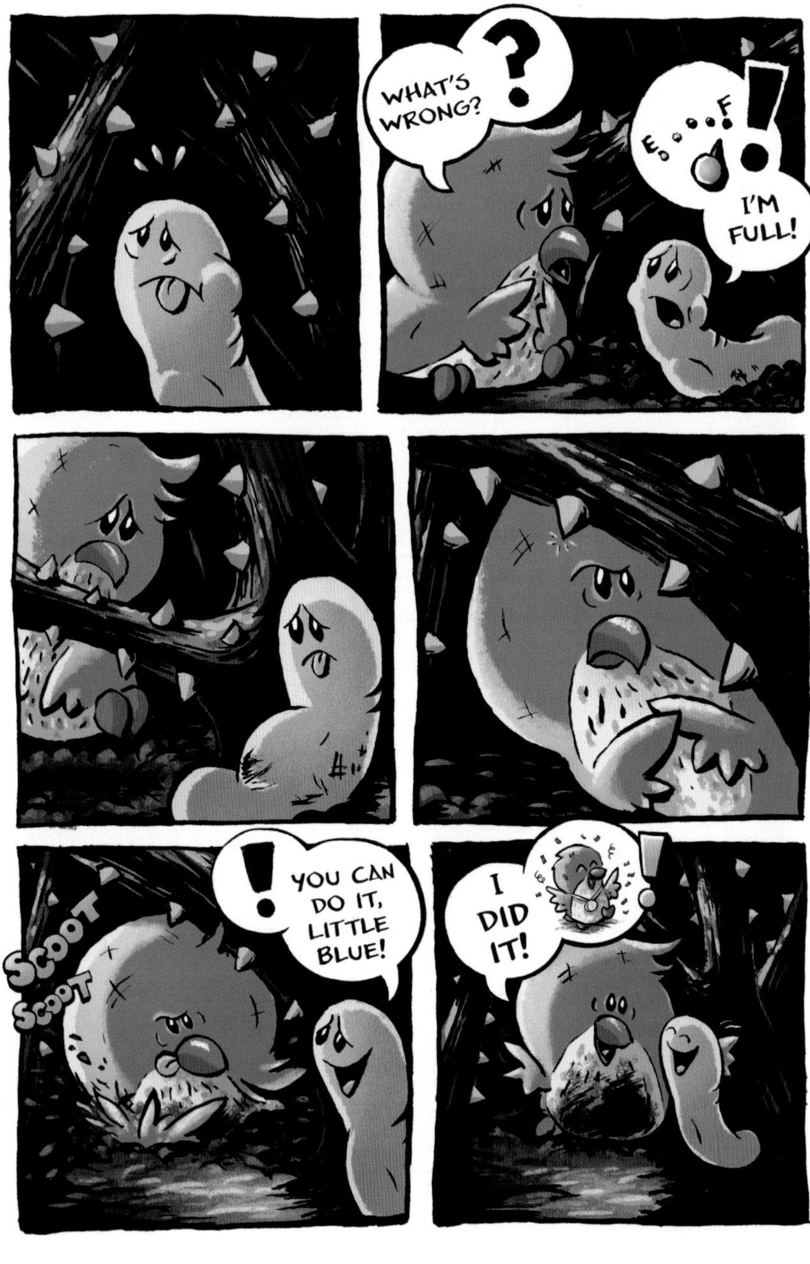
WHAT'S WRONG? ?
E...F! I'M FULL!
SCOOT SCOOT
! YOU CAN DO IT, LITTLE BLUE!
I DID IT! !

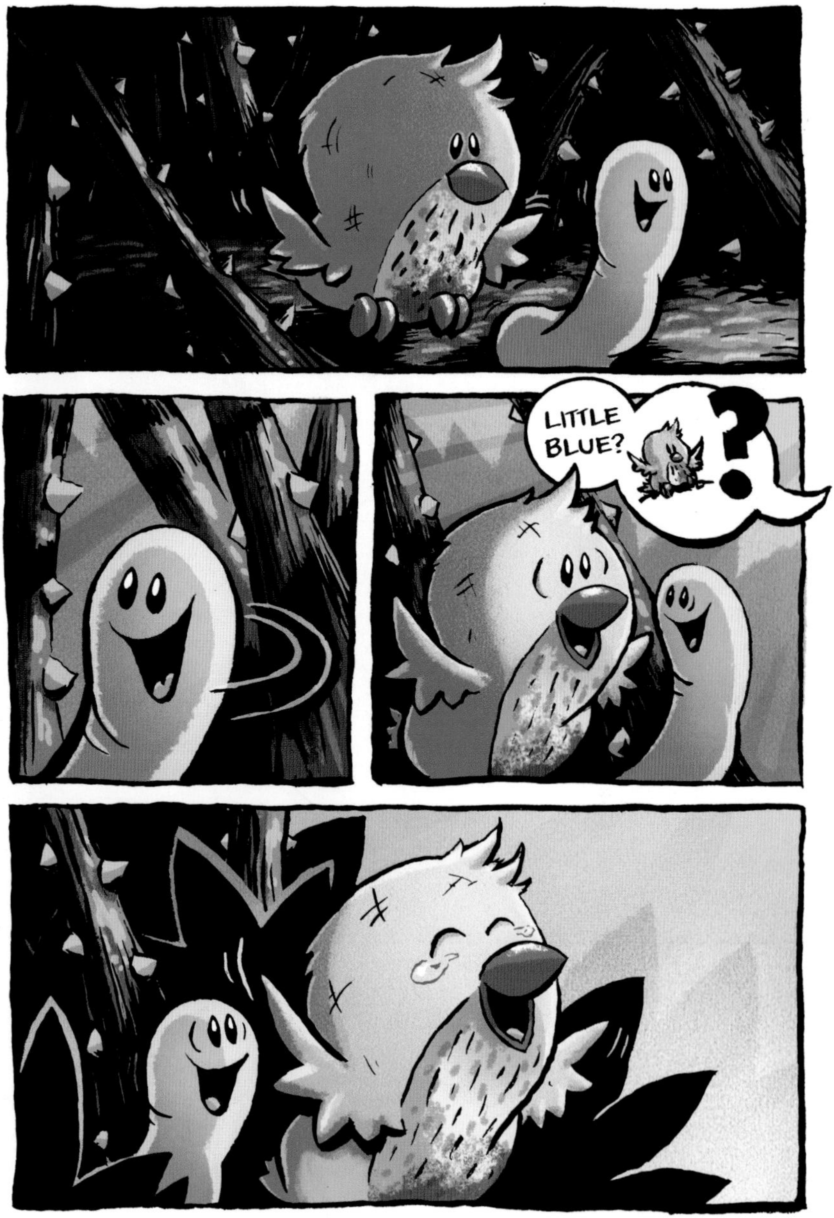
LITTLE BLUE?

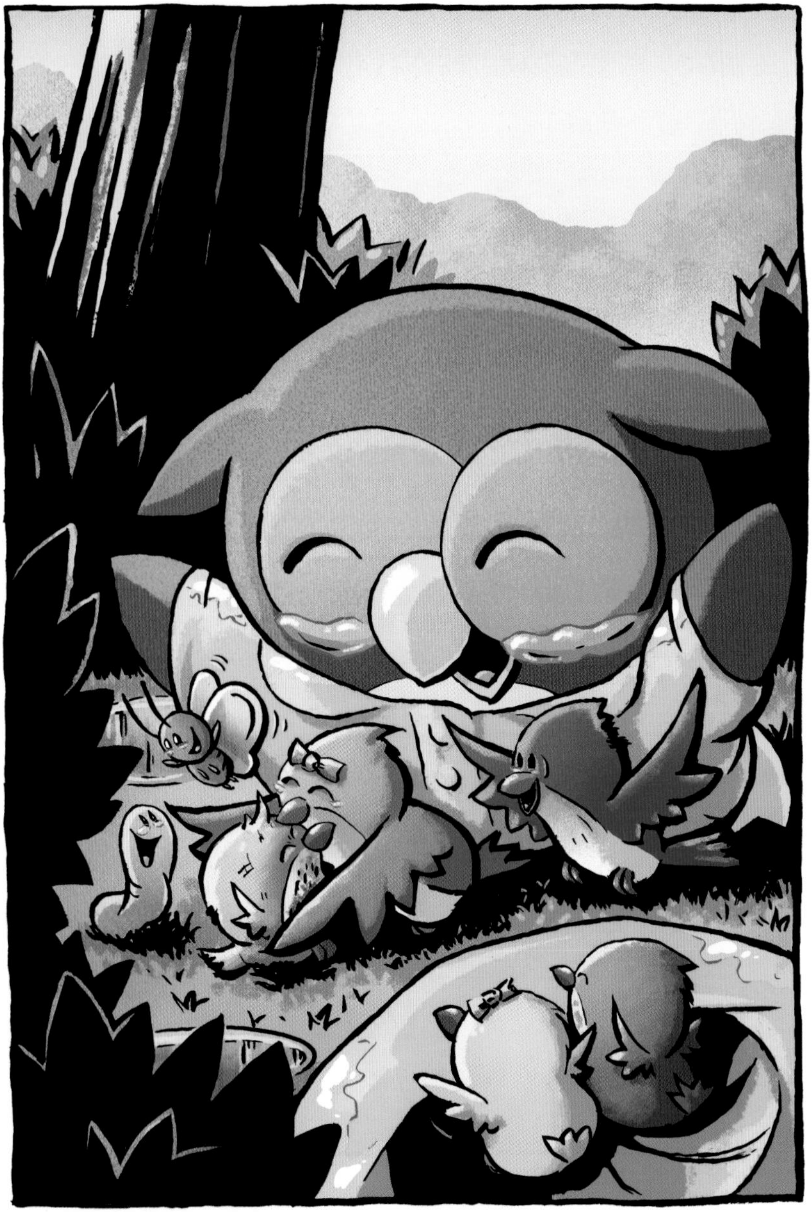

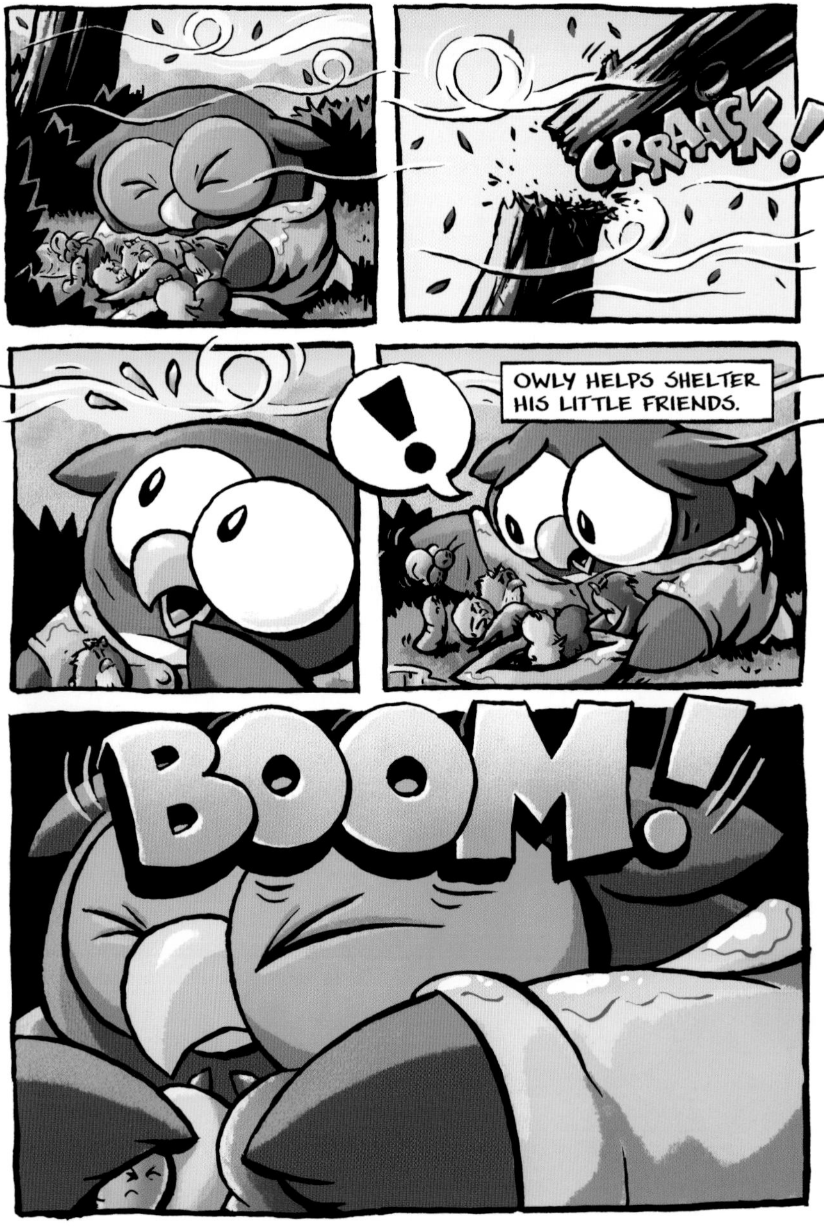
CRAACK!
!
OWLY HELPS SHELTER HIS LITTLE FRIENDS.
BOOM!!

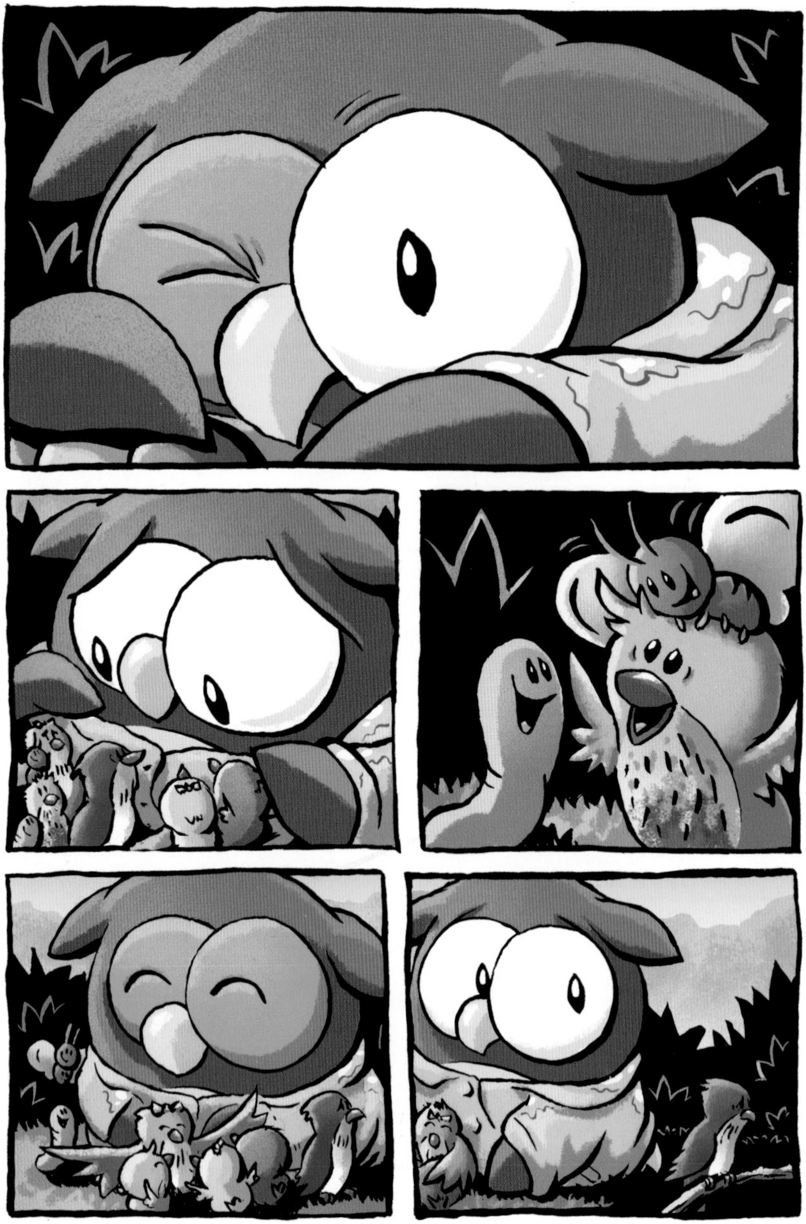

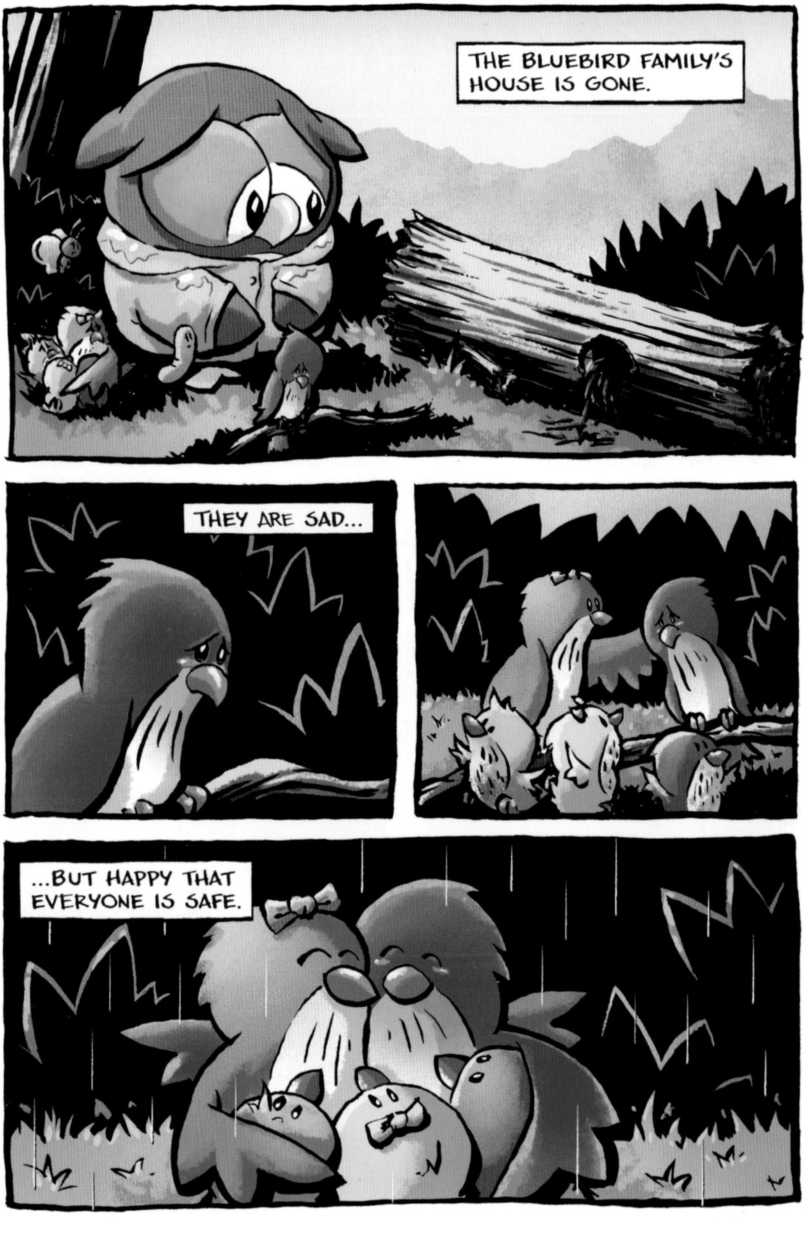
THE BLUEBIRD FAMILY'S HOUSE IS GONE.
THEY ARE SAD...
...BUT HAPPY THAT EVERYONE IS SAFE.

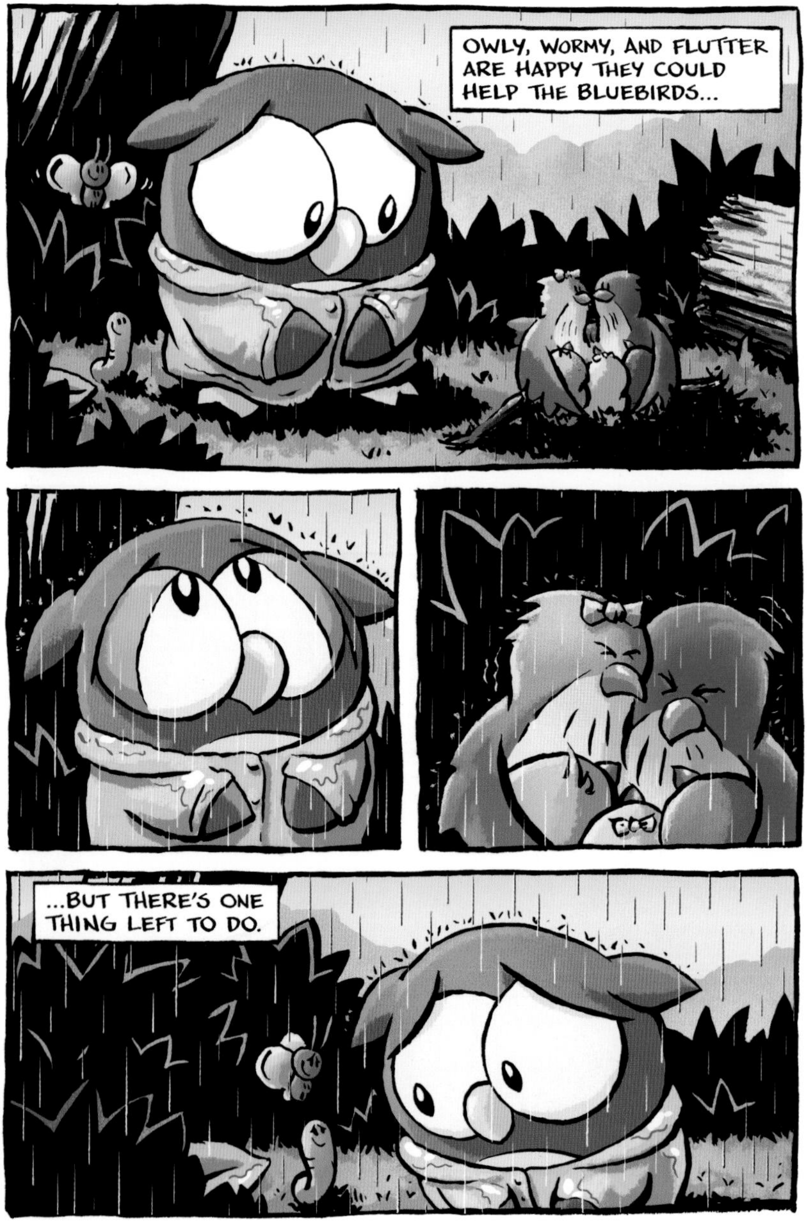
OWLY, WORMY, AND FLUTTER ARE HAPPY THEY COULD HELP THE BLUEBIRDS...
...BUT THERE'S ONE THING LEFT TO DO.

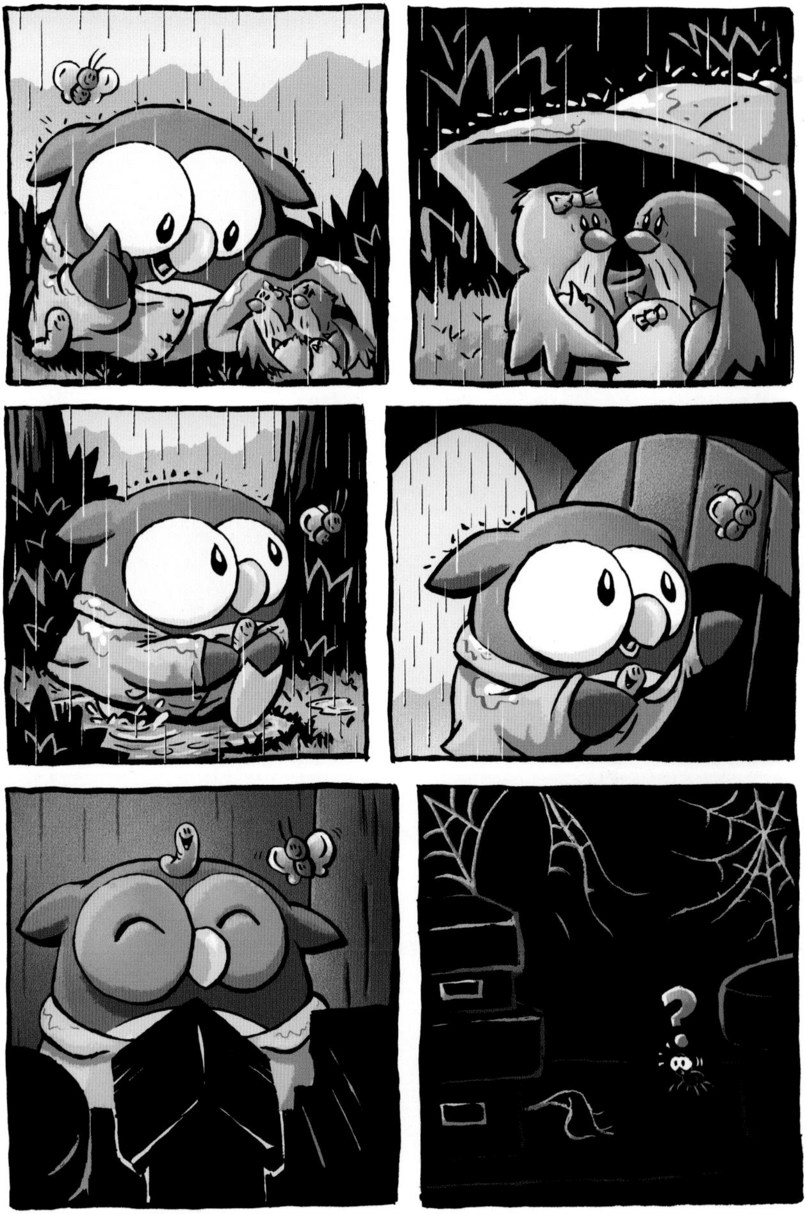
?

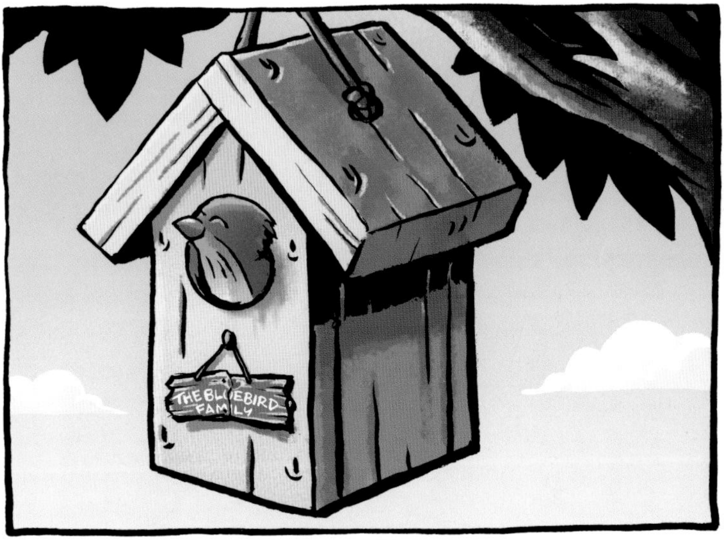
THE BLUEBIRD FAMILY

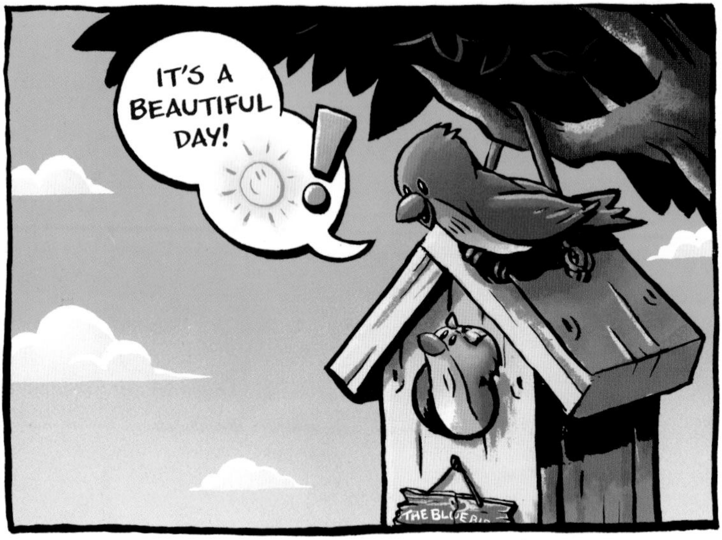
IT'S A BEAUTIFUL DAY!

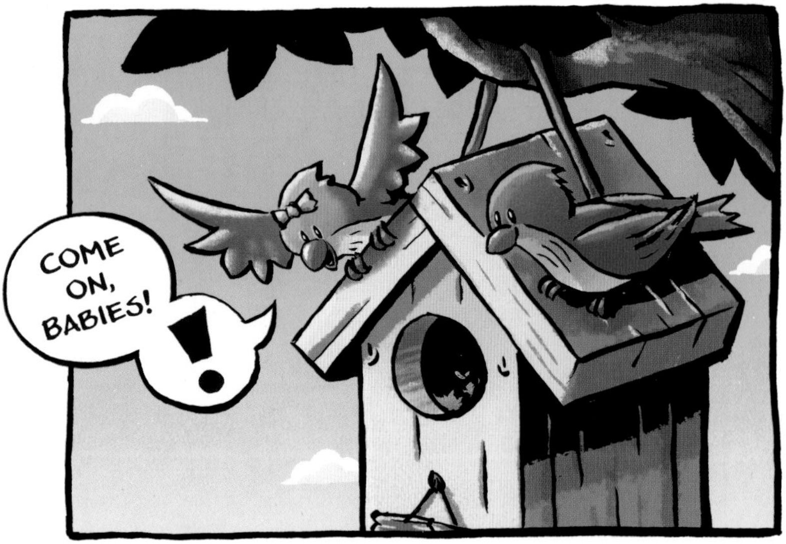
COME ON, BABIES!
!

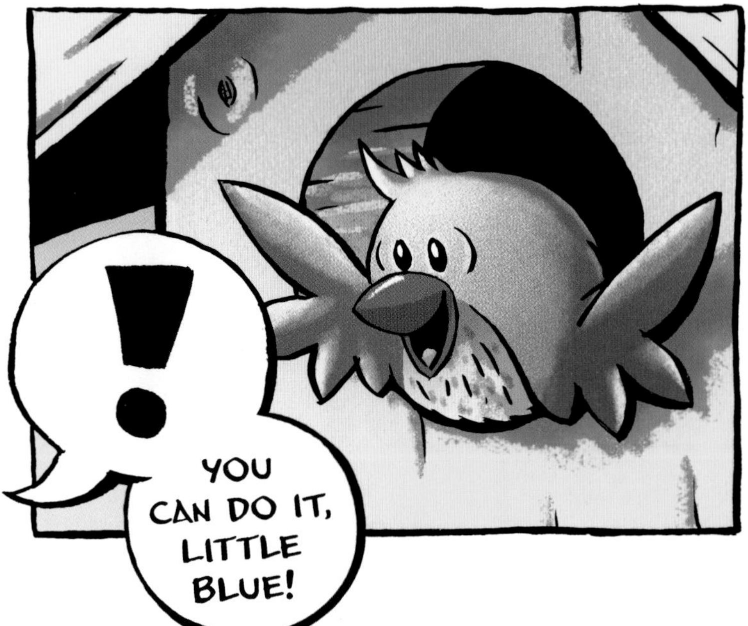
!
YOU CAN DO IT, LITTLE BLUE!

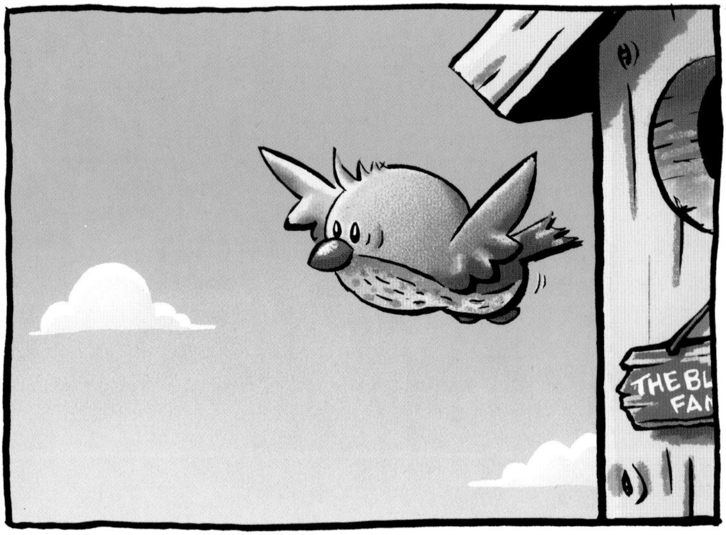
THE BL
FA

THE
END

Flutter, Wormy, and Little Blue
☺

MORE OWLY ADVENTURES TO COME!

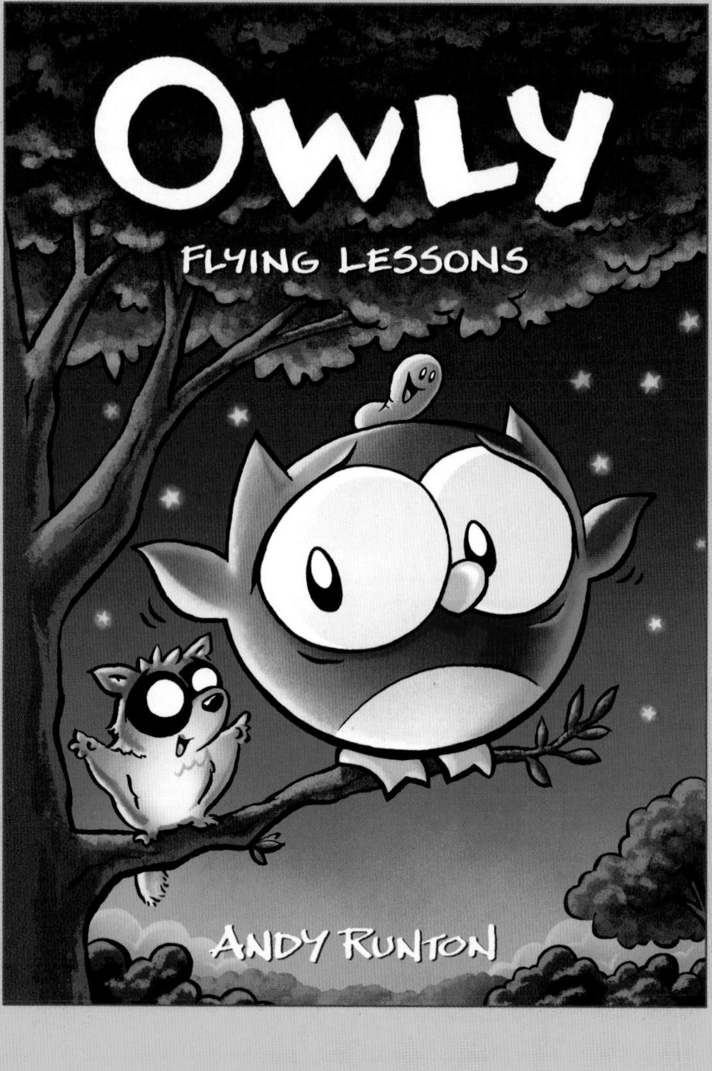
OWLY
FLYING LESSONS
ANDY RUNTON

SPECIAL THANKS
TO ALL OF THE OWLY FANS,
AND TO MY FAMILY AND FRIENDS
FOR THEIR INCREDIBLE SUPPORT!
IT MEANS THE WORLD TO ME! ᶜ"

THANK YOU TO RAINA
FOR ALWAYS BEING THERE FOR ME,
TO MY AGENT, BARRY, FOR CHAMPIONING OWLY,
AND TO DAVID, MEGAN, PHIL, AND EVERYONE
ON TEAM OWLY AT SCHOLASTIC GRAPHIX!
YOU'RE ALL AMAZING, AND I CAN'T THANK YOU
ENOUGH FOR YOUR ENTHUSIASM AND HARD WORK!

AN EXTRA SPECIAL THANK YOU TO MY MOM,
PATTY RUNTON, FOR ALL OF HER TIRELESS COLORING
ASSISTANCE ON THIS BOOK, FOR BEING THERE FOR ME,
FOR BEING MY BIGGEST FAN AND CHEERLEADER, AND
FOR BELIEVING IN ME AND OWLY WHEN WE WERE
STUCK IN THE RAIN FOR SO LONG.

AND THANK YOU, DEAR READER,
FOR SHARING OWLY'S ADVENTURES.
HERE'S TO MANY, MANY MORE!
THANK YOU!

ANDY RUNTON

is the award-winning creator of Owly, which has earned him multiple awards, including the Eisner Award for Best Publication for a Younger Audience. The Owly books have been praised for their "charm, wisdom, and warmth" by *Booklist*, and WIRED.com said they are "one of the best comics for kids around. Period." Andy lives in the greater Atlanta area, where he works full time as a writer and illustrator. Visit him online at andyrunton.com.

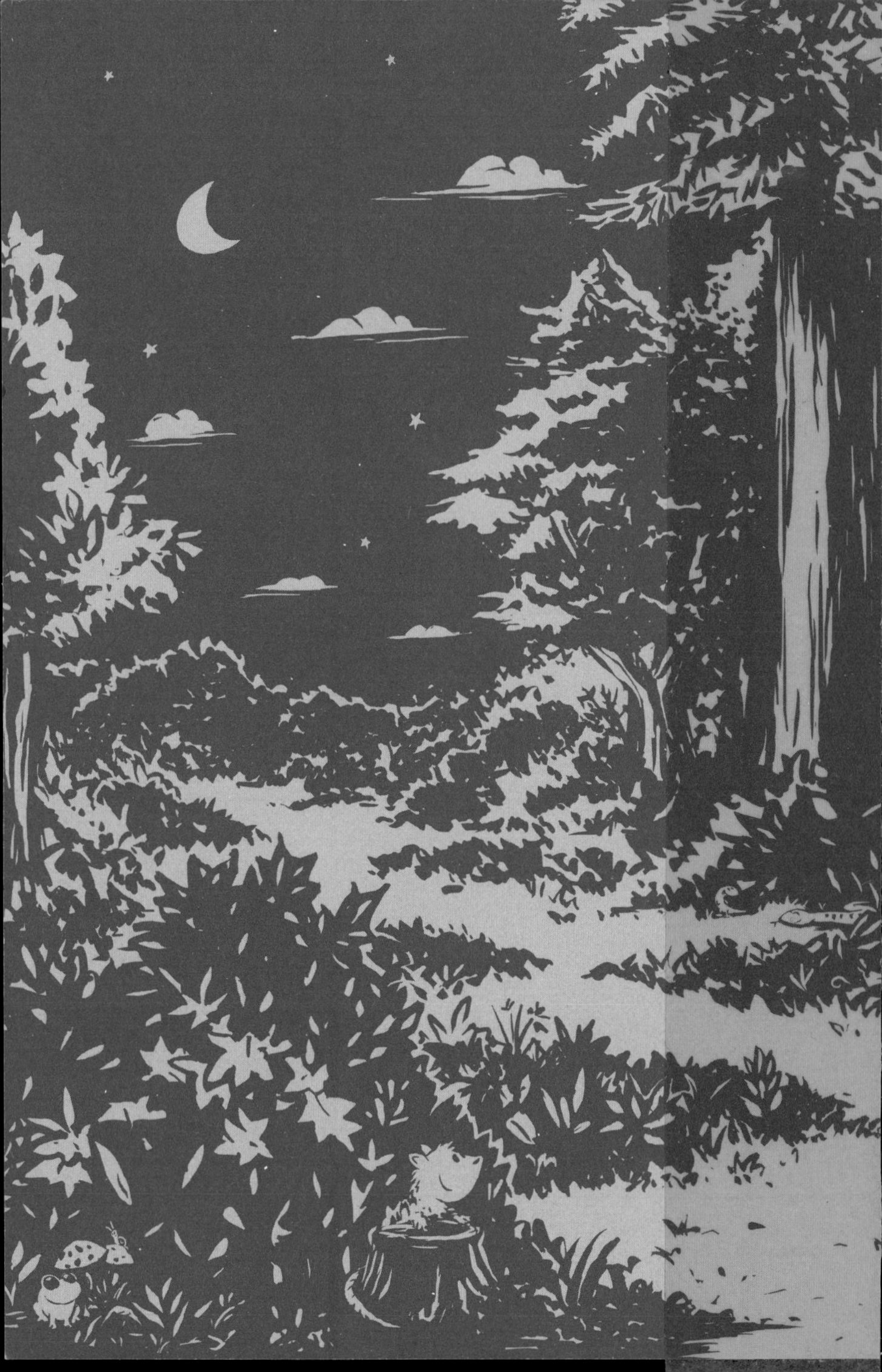